# Ladies Won't Wait

## PETER CHEYNEY

Ladies Won't Wait
Peter Cheyney
First published by William Collins, London,
England in 1951.
Also known as Cocktails and the Killer
This production Copyright © 2022
Cover by Mats Ingelborn
with photo from NejronPhoto, Shutterstock
ISBN paper: 978-91-89225-63-3
ISBN e-book: 978-91-89225-64-0
ISBN audiobook: 978-91-89225-62-6
Published by Yabot AB, Stockholm, 2022

# I. — JANEY

**EVEN** to-day I don't know very much about her. Which is a pity. I suppose if I knew her story I shouldn't spend so much time wondering about it. Somebody or other said that unsatisfied curiosity fed upon itself, and there's nothing that can supply food for thought like a mysterious woman who appears from nowhere, mixes herself up in one's life for a little while and then goes out of it. Especially if she happens to be beautiful.

In my own rather odd profession one is inclined to speculate a great deal about women. In terms of their peculiar effect upon people, and I say peculiar because no two men are affected in exactly the same way by women. If they were, life would be a great deal easier.

I suppose, really, Theodora St. Philippe must have been some sort of desperate idealist. She must have been—even if her ideals were a bit cock-eyed. Besides beauty, and that indefinable attraction which all women want to possess and so few do, she must have had brains and intelligence and a helluva lot of guts. I ought to have known from the first time I saw her that she was a rather special sort of person. I ought to have known. If I didn't it was because I was much too busy looking at her and wondering just who and what she was; when and how she'd acquired that strange quality of allure, that extraordinary grace....

Anyhow... she's had it and that's that. And in my profession it doesn't do too much good to spend your off-times in wondering about women who've had it. Especially those who've won it in the same way as you might easily win it yourself. One of these days!

I came away from the Pré-Catalan about five o'clock. I drove into the Champs Elysées, turned off and parked the car in the Rue Royale not far from Maxims. I had a drink in Maxims. I didn't want it, but I had it. It was so hot you could hardly breathe. July, if it is hot, is not the sort of month you'd pick to be in Paris.

When I came out I began to walk down the Rue Royale, and she was about ten paces in front of me. I tell you she was something! And because I was undecided in my mind and wasn't quite certain at that particular moment—I had just a few minutes to spare before my appointment with Olly—as to where I wanted to go or what I wanted to do, I just trailed along behind her, admiring the way she put her feet on the ground and that just too elegant sway with which she walked.

I thought she was marvellous. She turned into the Rue du Faubourg St. Honoré, and when I went round the corner after her I jerked my mind back to realities and thought it was about time I went home. I suppose I forgot Olly for the time being, which was strange, because I'd had Olly in the back of my head for the last two hours. If it hadn't been for my goddam sex curiosity maybe I'd have been back minutes before. Anyway, I started to walk, thinking about the woman. I crossed the Faubourg; turned into a side street. Then, a few minutes afterwards, I saw it. A beret of a peculiar shade of blue lying in the gutter, looking just as if it had been run over, which funnily enough it had been, and

                                          Peter Cheyney

with the oil stain on the side.

I thought: That's Olly's beret. I didn't like it. I went round the corner and there was the flic with his note-book out, and two or three people talking to him all at once—talking rapidly and rather vehemently, which was quite unnecessary since nobody seemed to know anything at all about it.

It was Olly all right. I spoke to the flic. As far as he could ascertain, Olly, who by the way was a very tough Frenchman of nearly sixty, had been leaning up against the wall, smoking a cigarette and doing nothing in particular. The next time the flic passed, which was some five minutes later, Olly was lying in the gutter in the quiet street. He was dead... a hit and run driver, apparently. They had taken the body away.

I thought it was a bit hard that Olly, with his ex-periences in the war, his toughness, his astuteness and the courage he brought to life, should finish like that. I talked to the flic for a few minutes and I went off.

I started to walk round the streets, thinking about Olly, wondering. Then I went back to Maxims and had a drink. I drank a brandy cocktail and leaned up against the bar with my mind running around the blue beret with the oil stain on it lying in the gutter, and looking in some strange way almost animate, rather as if it want-ed to get up and talk to me. I ordered another brandy cocktail, paid for it and didn't drink it.

I went back and found the beret was still there. I picked it up. I don't know why I wanted to do that, but I did it. Then I started to meander round the streets. I was walking more or less in a circle, which was what I wanted to do. After a while I thought I had as much chance of seeing what I wanted to as finding a needle in a haystack, and just as I came to this conclusion I saw the needle!

It was parked in front of me. It was a 6/15 Citroen car which, if you know anything about Paris, is not at all unusual. They grow on gooseberry bushes there. The streets are full of them.

But I knew this one. I could see the small cut in the near- side wing that had broken open after the wing had been newly planished. I walked over to the car and slipped my hand under the driver's door-handle. And there was the groove on the underneath side of the handle. So I knew who the car belonged to. And I wondered what the hell it was doing there.

And then I saw the other thing, which was the front number plate. And there was the number on it as large as life, and the egg who had painted the number on it had been too lazy to get a new plate. He'd painted over the old number. You could see the vague outlines of the original number underneath. So it was Rockie's car originally, which I thought, having regard to this and that, was very funny.

I started walking again; finished up looking in the window of Lanvin's men's shop in the Faubourg. But I wasn't looking at anything. I was smoking a cigarette without tasting it and thinking about the car and Olly. When I turned away from the window, having come to the conclusion that looking in shirt shop windows wasn't a paying proposition, I saw the woman coming down the Faubourg towards me. I had another look at her.

                                        Peter Cheyney

I didn't think she was French. In spite of what she'd got she was English. And she looked a very nice woman when you looked at her. And as she swayed past me she gave me the eye. I thought: Well... well...! I watched her as she floated down the street a little way and then stopped and looked into a perfumery shop, to give me a chance to make my approach, I supposed.

But I wasn't sure and you have to be sure about a thing like that. I'd spent so long running the garage, and trying to kid everybody that that was my job, that I didn't even think, at the moment, that she might have some sort ulterior motive. Of course, I should have thought of it, and probably would have, except that three-quarters of my mind was concerned with Olly and the business of his getting himself rubbed out in such an annoying manner.

So I thought to hell with it! I crossed the street; went back to where I had parked the car and drove slowly home. I went up the two flights of stairs and pushed the door open; went into the bedroom; lay down on the bed; looked at the ceiling and thought where do we go from here?

But not for long! I heard somebody at the front door and bawled: "Come in...."

A moment later somebody pushed the bedroom door open and Janey came in.

Janey leaned against the wall and looked at me with mischievous blue eyes. He was tall, slim, rangey, with a particular charm which isn't easy to describe.

He wasn't good-looking, but he was very attractive. Women went for him in a big way. His face was odd.

It missed being good-looking by a near margin. And his eyes were very good. They were strange eyes—deep, sometimes mischievous, sometimes smiling in a cold sort of way. He walked with a peculiar, casual grace and his clothes—no matter how old they were—hung on him perfectly. He would have looked well-dressed in an old sack.

His name was Everard Mailey Jane. Someone told me he came of an antique family, but some woman had christened him "Janey," and it stuck. It suited him. He seemed to have money of his own, and did what he thought interesting jobs about the world. He was an Englishman, but had fought with the Americans in World War II and collected a couple of gongs. He had also done a little airplane testing for them, and had a share in a business somewhere or other.

I met him in Frankfurt two years ago.

He said with a grin: "You old bastard. Lying on the bed and looking at the ceiling and smoking. What are you plotting... some woman I'll bet?"

I said: "You don't know how right you are. I wish to God I hadn't seen her!"

He raised his eyebrows. "So... it's like that. What did she do? Did she bite you?"

"No... not exactly. She was what the Americans call a looker and I went on looking too long...."

"And you missed an appointment?" he said.

I nodded. I told him about the woman.

He pushed himself away from the wall; lighted a cigarette; began to walk about the room looking at the weird pictures that I'd acquired with the apartment.

                                        Peter Cheyney

He asked: "What was she like?"

I said: "She was tall and slim, and she had one hell of a figure, and the sort of legs that you dream about. She had a way of walking, too... you know, Janey. And her clothes were something. She was wearing a chartreuse shangtung tailored coat and skirt, with black gloves and a black shiny sailor hat and patent leather sandals with the right sort of heel, and sheer nylons. I think that woman was very intriguing, Janey."

He yawned. "Yes? Most women are intriguing for some reason or other, aren't they?"

I said: "I suppose so. But according to the kind of quality that makes them intriguing. A woman might be intriguing because she had no ears. That wouldn't make her attractive, would it, Janey?"

He said: "No. Well, what's so marvellous about this woman you saw?"

"I don't know. She was perfectly dressed. She looked as if she was English. She looked as if she might have been well-bred. But there was something rather odd about her. She gave me the impression that she was trying to pick me up."

He yawned again. "That wouldn't make her intriguing, would it? Except to you, perhaps. So she tried to pick you up?"

I said: "Maybe. Well..." I got off the bed. "That's a point which will remain unsettled. I don't propose to ask her."

"This description rather reminds me of a woman I met in Frankfurt," said Janey. "I'll have to tell you about her." He looked at his strap-watch. "D'you know what

the time is? It's six o'clock. I think we should go somewhere and have a drink, don't you?"

I looked at him. I thought to myself: I wonder what's
on your mind; what you're trying to do. I stood there
smiling, looking at Janey and wondering just how deep
those mischievous smiling eyes of his were; how far the
pools behind them extended into the brain and what
was going on inside that brain. I thought to myself: I
think you're a son-of-a-bitch and if you are I'm going
to have you, Janey.

I grinned at him. I said: "I think it's a hell of an idea.
Let's go and have a drink."

We went downstairs and walked for a bit. We went
into Charles' Bar. Janey said he liked the atmosphere.
We drank two large whiskies and sodas. I'd just ordered
another round when a man came in. He came across.

He said: "Hallo, Janey. How's it going with you?"

He was short and thin. He had high cheek bones
and a pronounced pallor. He looked as if he might have
been slightly tubercular or something like that. He had
a mean sort of face with long, narrow eyes, but the effect
was lightened by an almost permanent smile about his
mouth.

Janey said: "Not too bad. How does it go with you?"
He turned to me. "This is a friend of mine. His name's
Marcini. A most peculiar specimen." He grinned pleas-
antly. "I don't know who he is or what he does or why,
but wherever I go I meet him. He always has enough
money in his pocket to buy me an expensive drink. He
never talks about himself. When he asks questions you
never know he's doing it." He said to Marcini: "This is

                                    Peter Cheyney

Michael Kells."

Marcini looked at me. He said, with the slightest touch of a foreign accent: "I think you're a very fine specimen, Kells." He stepped back and looked me over. "I should say your weight's nearly two hundred pounds. In spite of that you look thin. So I should think most of it was muscle. You've nice eyes, a tough jaw, very good teeth and women would like your hair. Do you know, Kells, I think women might like a lot of you. Yes, I should think you're very attractive to women. Wouldn't you think so, Janey?"

The waiter brought our drinks. I told him to bring another.

Janey said to Marcini: "You're telling me. This egg has been ruined by women so many times that the process doesn't even affect him any more. Why they fall for him I don't know. Perhaps it's because he doesn't talk a lot. He's always finding beautiful women or rather he thinks he's finding them. Usually they find him."

Marcini said: "That's how it goes. For me... I'm always very unlucky with them. I don't like women except very occasionally. When I meet one, if I do like her, she doesn't like me. I suppose I'm unfortunate."

"Not necessarily," I said.

He nodded. "You might be right," he conceded. "I remember once in Mexico City I had a little trouble with a woman—she was charming and good-looking, also intelligent, which I thought was unique. She came to the conclusion that I had two-timed her with a hat-check girl at a night club. So she made an appointment with me and brought a small automatic pistol with her.

When she saw me approaching she produced the pistol and fired at me. She missed me and killed her husband who was following me. A most distressing business."

I asked: "Why? Think of the money and trouble you saved yourself. Who was the Chinese philosopher who said that the only woman a man really desired was the one he couldn't get?"

Janey said: "Yes, that boy knew his stuff whoever he was." He drank some whisky. He went on: "How's the garage going, Mike?"

"It's all right," I told him. "In point of fact it was a very good idea of mine. It's become a sheet anchor to me, that garage."

"So you're making money?" asked Janey.

I nodded. "A little. And it keeps me out of mischief."

There was a little silence; then Janey said: "How's that old boy who used to get around with you? I saw him once or twice in Frankfurt. I believe you mentioned the garage idea to him. Then you told him that if you went through with it you'd put him in charge."

I said: "You mean Olly—the Frenchman."

"Yes. How's Olly?"

I lighted a cigarette. I said: "He's dead. A hit and run driver got him this evening—about an hour ago—in a quiet street. Just knocked him down and killed him. I arrived a few minutes after it had happened."

Janey said: "Good God! What a weird egg you are. You never said a word about it to me."

"Why should I, Janey? What's the good of talking about a thing like that? If a man's dead, he's dead."

He said: "Well, goddam it, he was running the garage

                                    

for you, wasn't he?"

"Maybe... There'll be another Olly. There must be lots of people in France looking for garage managers' jobs."

He looked at Marcini and grinned. "You see, he's tough. That's why he gets on. He just doesn't take any notice of a little thing like somebody's death." He went on: "I wonder if they'll get the motorist who did it. It's a pretty lousy thing to hit a man and not stop."

I said: "I think so, too."

"I think this conversation should be changed," said Marcini. "I find talking about death is not very happy. There are other things to talk about."

"All right," said Janey. "There's his latest woman. Let's talk about her."

Marcini raised his eyebrows. "What woman?"

Janey said: "He tells me when he came out of Maxims—mark you, I don't know how many brandy cocktails he'd had—floating down the Rue Royale in front of him is a most devastating piece. She was so good that the boy friend had to go after her half-way down the Faubourg St. Honoré. He just had to go on looking."

Marcini said languidly: "Was that all?"

"Yes, that's what he says. That was all. She disappeared into thin air. The only pleasure he got out of this brief encounter was that he missed an appointment."

Marcini laughed. "Too bad. I'll make a guess that the appointment he missed was with an even more beautiful woman and, because he didn't keep it, when he did arrive she was gone. Isn't that true, Kells? Isn't that the story?"

I said: "No. I hadn't an appointment with a beautiful woman. I had an appointment with Olly. If it hadn't been for the baby with the lovely figure I'd have kept it, and the probability is that Olly would still have been alive."

Marcini shrugged his shoulders. "That is how it goes. That is life. Walking about Paris at this moment, or probably drinking a cocktail, is this lovely woman who is indirectly responsible for the death of Kells' garage manager. And she doesn't even know it. I wonder what would happen if somebody went up to her and told her about it. I wonder if she'd even be sorry."

I said: "How do I know? I don't know and I don't care very much."

Marcini said: "This conversation is still on a rather sombre note. I'm going to buy another drink."

I said: "I don't like drinking too much spirits in hot weather, so I'll have a large whisky and soda with some ice in it."

Marcini gave the order.

Janey said: "Mike, did you ever come across Rockie when you were in Frankfurt?"

I looked at him. "Rockie...? Who's Rockie?"

He said: "You've answered my question. I see you couldn't have met him. He's one of the most amusing types—almost a relic of the past."

I asked: "Why is he a relic?"

He said: "I think he's the world's best play-boy. Rockie is about thirty—certainly not thirty-five. He has a lot of money, which is unusual, and it's good money because it comes from America. I've never known a man drink so much, spend so much money and get so much fun out of it as Rockie."

I asked: "Did he get a lot of fun in Germany? I shouldn't have thought that Frankfurt was the place for a lot of fun—not that sort of fun—at the moment."

He said: "He had fun, anyway. The reason I mentioned his name, Mike, was because if you'd known him you might have known his sister. Talking about beautiful women you brought to my mind the name. I should think Rockie's sister is the loveliest thing I've ever seen."

I yawned. "That's O.K. by me. And what does she do. Is she a play-girl?"

He shook his head. "She's delightful... as sensible as he's stupid. She lives in Sussex in England. She has an old manor house and a farm. She's the sort of person who'd drive you crazy, Mike."

I grinned at him. "Oh, yes... why?"

He said: "Well, she knows her own mind. She's poised. I should say she's quite clever in a quiet sort of way. And she wouldn't stand for any damned nonsense from you."

"Why should she? I don't even know her, and I don't want to."

Marcini said: "We talk about dead garage foremen and we talk about beautiful women who have been pursued by Kells and beautiful women who live in Sussex, and I don't think it's at all interesting."

I asked: "What would you like to talk about?"

"I don't like talking," said Marcini. "I like listening."

I said: "Well, what would you like to listen to?"

"That's the joke... I don't know."

We finished the drinks.

Marcini asked: "Well, what... if anything... are we going to do?"

Janey said: "I'm game for anything. I'm only here for two or three days; then I'm going off on my travels."

I asked: "Where are you going to, Janey?"

"I don't know," he said. "I thought I might go back to Germany. There's a very interesting little Fräulein I know in Frankfurt, in spite of what you think about it, Mike. What are you going to do?"

I said: "I'm going back to England in a day or two I think."

Janey began to laugh. "What did I tell you? All I have to do is to tell him about a lovely lady in Sussex and he makes up his mind to go back to England."

I said: "Nuts!"

Marcini shook his head. "You're quite wrong, Janey. I don't think his technique would be so hurried."

I picked up my hat. "Well, I'll be seeing you two some time or other some place. You know where to find me, Janey. You found me a little earlier." I stubbed out my cigarette. "By the way, how did you know my address?"

He said: "I got it at The Travellers' Club."

"Did you? Who gave it to you—the hall porter?"

"Of course. Who else?"

I didn't say anything for a moment, then: "Well... until next time...."

I went out of the bar.

                                    Peter Cheyney

I stood for a moment on the pavement outside, undecided. Then I began to walk slowly towards Maxims. I walked into the Faubourg St. Honoré, round the corner into the Rue Royale. I began to meander down the right hand side of the street. When I got within sight of Maxims I saw her. She was standing under the awning and she wasn't the sort of person who stood under awnings outside Maxims. It was my girl friend of the early evening. She looked just as cool; just as collected.

As I approached her she turned; moved round in the direction of the Place de la Concorde. The way she walked was still very attractive. When I got round the corner she was buying a newspaper from the newsvendor. There was the usual crowd milling about; the usual traffic; the usual bunch of people trying to get across the street. I bought a newspaper. I opened it; said out of the corner of my mouth:

"You wouldn't be interested in me or anything, would you, Madame? Or would it be Mademoiselle?"

She said: "Why not, M'sieu? The world is a very small place. And it isn't often one sees a man quite as attractive as you are."

"Thank you for nothing. A very good line of talk."

She said: "Perhaps it isn't even talk."

I asked: "If it isn't, what is it?"

She said quietly: "M'sieu... ladies won't wait. They believe more in action."

"And the address?" I queried.

She said: "2 bis Place des Roses—not too far from the Etoile. On the second floor. Be unostentatious."

"You'd be surprised. I'll be there. About eleven, when

it's dark. Expect me. Au revoir."

She walked a few yards; signalled a cab. I thought: Well, that's that. But I wasn't surprised.

I'm not often surprised.

I looked at my strap-watch. It was eight o'clock. I began to walk up the Champs Elysées towards The Travellers' Club. Most of the time I was thinking about the woman. The Old Man seemed to be finding 'em these days. I wondered what her particular assignment was, or whether it was merely to contact me. In the last year or so the Old Man had become very careful. During the years I had worked for him I'd never known him to be so careful. Personally, I think he was right. These days you never know where you are. Most of Europe is a battle-ground of espionage agents, intelligence people, double agents and double-double agents; everybody trying to double-cross each other like hell and some-times getting away with it. The Old Man had done his best to try and keep the book straight by handing out a few code words for every few months, so that when agents who were unknown to each other met, there was no question about identities; there was no need to carry those minute identifications which we'd used during the war. The code was much better and the one for July-August was 'Ladies won't wait.' Directly she'd spo-ken the words I realised from the very look of her that she was the sort of girl the Old Man would choose—a woman who looked like anything butan agent.

I began to think about Janey; Marcini. Some of the things I thought were extremely improbable, if not im-possible. But life's like that. I should think during the

                                          Peter Cheyney

last ten years everything had happened which was considered impossible, and people who don't believe in impossibilities these days ought to go and bury themselves somewhere quietly. They'd find life easier that way.

I went into The Travellers' Club and talked to Jacques, the head porter. I said: "Jacques, has Mr. Jane been in to-day asking for me? I expected a message from him."

He said: "No, M'sieu. 'E 'as not been in. I 'ave been on duty all day."

I thought: "So that's that!" In other words Janey hadn't been into The Travellers' Club. He hadn't got my address from Jacques, and he had some reason for concealing where he had got the information from. I didn't think that was quite so good, and began to believe a little more in impossibilities.

I came out of the Club; took a cab; drove back to my apartment. I took off my coat; went into the bathroom and dipped my head and hands in cold water. Then I mixed a long whisky and soda with a lump of ice; opened the window in my sitting-room; sat in an easy-chair with my feet up on the window ledge, breathing the somewhat cooler air, and chewing over things.

What did I know about Janey? Nothing very much. I knew less about Marcini, whom I had met for the first time that evening. But I was concentrating on Janey. He was one of those people who expected to be valued on his looks, and most people valued him that way. He was popular; had money or was considered to have money; was seen all over the place; was an athlete and a good sportsman. People took him at his face value. I'd done that myself, not because I'm careless—because I'm far from that—but because there was no reason why I should bother about him. I'd run into him in Frankfurt a half a dozen times.

I went over the sequence of events in my mind—the events of the early evening. Janey arrived at my apartment. He said he was only in Paris for two or three days. He was driving Rockie's old car. Someone had painted out the original number and the number of Janey's car, which I remembered because I've a trained memory for that sort of thing and he was driving the car in Frankfurt, had been painted over the old one—pretty carelessly, too.

From some source Janey had got the address of my apartment, which very few people knew, and which wasn't in the telephone directory. He told me he had got it from Jacques at The Travellers' Club, which was a lie, which meant he didn't want me to know where he'd got it from. Then he brought up Rockie's name in the course of conversation. I didn't fall for that one. I professed to know nothing about Rockie. But he felt he ought to have a reason for bringing it up, so he told me about Rockie's sister. He put the idea into my head that I was the sort of man who might go over to England to see her. Maybe he wanted me to do that. I shrugged my shoulders. At the moment it was a little difficult to know what anybody wanted.

He wanted a drink and specifically he wanted to go to Charles' Bar. And a couple of minutes afterwards his friend Marcini arrived. This could have been accidental of course. It might have been just one of those

                    Peter Cheyney

coincidences and it might not have been. It might be that he'd insisted on going to Charles' Bar because he wanted Marcini to identify me. Maybe he knew what my job was. Maybe he knew that I'd been working for the Old Man for years. If he did, where had he got the information from?

Then, on top of all this, there was my mysterious lady friend, who was also working for the Old Man; who'd been doing her best to get me to pick her up at the time when I came out of Maxims. She must have done a lot of walking that afternoon. And why would she use such a process? Only because she didn't want to use my telephone number to make an appointment, and because she didn't want to come round to my apartment. Because the Old Man knew where I was. He knew the address of my apartment and the address of the garage I used for a front in Paris. And the only reason that she wouldn't phone or come round to the apartment was because such a process would be dangerous, which meant that something was breaking.

Of course it could be all one peculiar set of coincidences. But I'd found that car—Rockie's Citroen—near the place where Olly was killed in the side street. Janey was driving that car. He'd told me a lie about how he'd found out where I was, and he wanted to go to Charles' Bar because he liked Charles' Bar, and Marcini had come in purely by chance. It could have been like that, but I didn't believe it was like that. I had a hunch.

I drank my drink slowly; asked myself what I was worrying about. Probably the solution of the whole business lay in the hands of Madame, whom I intended to see later in the evening. I'd probably get the whole story from her, or at least a bearing on it. I'd find out what the Old Man wanted.

I put on my coat and went out. I stopped a taxicab and told him to drive to the garage at the end of the Rue de la Chappelle. When I got there, Le Fevre—the mechanic on late duty—was just closing up. I told him to wait a minute before he pulled down the shutter; walked across the floor of the garage into Olly's little glass-fronted office in the corner. Lying on the oil-stained table was Olly's day-book—the book in which he kept a record of daily transactions. I opened it.

There it was. '3.30 R.F. 6347. Oil, Gas, Tyres.'

I thought: That ties it up. I began to believe that my guess was right. That was the number of Janey's car—the new number that had been painted over Rockie's old one. So at 3.30 that afternoon Janey had driven into the garage, bought petrol, checked his oil and had the tyres filled. I could imagine the scene. Maybe the other two mechanics had been busy. Olly had put the air into the tyres himself. I visualised him kneeling down fitting the air tube on to the near-side front wheel. From that position, if he looked up, he could see that peculiar groove under the driver's door-handle.

Oily would be on that like a knife. He knew that was Rockie's car. He had probably spoken to Janey about it; asked him where he'd got the car. And Janey had real-ised that he'd got to do something about it. Janey had realised that somehow Olly was to be prevented from seeing me and talking to me about that car. He'd gone off and hung about somewhere in the neighbourhood;

                    Peter Cheyney

waited until he'd seen Olly leave the garage; followed him. When Olly had gone into the side street, stretching his legs while he was waiting for me to turn up, Janey had taken his chance, run him down and made a certainty of him. Maybe he'd finished him off with a spanner or something. Nobody was going to worry very much. There are lots of street accidents in France. Then, quite calmly, he'd driven his car round the corner; left it there and slid off quickly before anybody came across Olly. After which he'd thought he'd better get a move on and see me, and bring up Rockie's name.

Maybe he thought I'd tell him I'd known Rockie for years; that he was a supreme actor, a play-boy, drinking and slinging money about all over Europe. Whilst all the time, underneath, he was one of the finest agents the Old Man had ever had and a particularly good friend of mine.

I said good night to Le Fevre; took a cab back to my apartment. I had another drink. I thought to myself: Well, if I'm right about you, Janey, I'll fix you one day. By God, I will...! Because—not that it mattered—I was rather fond of Olly. We'd been through the war together. He was a good egg. I thought it wasn't so hot that he should die in such a very uninteresting manner.

**I PASSED** the time until eleven o'clock by having a cold bath and changing my clothes. At eleven o'clock it was dark. I walked round to the Place des Roses, because I didn't think I'd chance taking a taxi-cab. It was a nice place. The Place des Roses was a long, narrow cul-de-sac formed by the backs of delightful old- fashioned buildings. The end of the cul-de-sac was 2 bis—a charming house with creeper, which looked as if somebody had omitted to fill in the end of the cul-de-sac and had thought suddenly of putting a house there.

I lighted a cigarette. I began to walk slowly round the cul- de-sac. I was wondering, I suppose, about the woman, wondering what she had to tell me. I thought it must be important. Yet I didn't know why. I shrugged my shoulders. This woman intrigued me. Quite apart from whatever business she had with me I thought she was a superb-looking person—one of the sort of women that most men spend their time thinking about—in imagination, if not in reality. When I'd finished the cigarette I threw the stub away and went back to the house.

The front door was open. Inside was an indicator which showed that the ground floor was the consulting room of a Doctor Simon, the first floor an agency office and the second floor the apartment of Madame St. Philippe. I thought I'd try that. I went up the stairs slowly. They were wooden and uncarpeted but very well cleaned, and my footsteps echoed strangely in the house, which had an atmosphere of strange emptiness.

When I arrived at the second floor the entrance door was in front of me. There was a nicely engraved card, with "Madame Theodora St. Philippe" on it, pinned to the door with a drawing-pin. I knocked, and the process opened the door, which was off the latch. I went in.

A small square hall, quite well-furnished, was lit by a shaded electric lamp. There was a door in front of me, a door to the left and a door to the right. I knocked at the door in front of me and went in. The room was large with indications of good taste—a woman's taste. There was a great bowl of roses on a walnut table in the centre of the room. At the end of the room on the right was a door. It was just ajar.

A woman's voice called softly in English: "Is that you, Mr. Kells?"

I said: "Yes."

The voice said: "Just a minute and I will be with you."

I put my hat on the table; smelled the roses; sat down in one of the big chairs by the fireplace. I lighted a cigarette. I imagined that my new colleague Madame St. Philippe had become tired of waiting and had decided to bath and change. I wondered what she would be wearing. I thought, having regard to her appearance of the earlier evening, that whatever she wore she'd look pretty good. I went on thinking about this for quite a bit. Then I called: "Madame...."

There was no answer. I got up; walked across to the door, tapped on it and went in. The room was in darkness. I fumbled about and found the switch by the door; flicked it on.

It wasn't at all nice... not a bit. She was lying on the bed. One handsome silk-clad leg was hanging over the side; the other foot touching the floor. The top of her well-shaped head was smashed in. It looked to me as if she had been getting off the bed when she'd been hit.

I went over to the bed and looked at her. She wasn't at all pretty—not now. The bed, which had a pink coverlet, and the frilled pillows, were in a hell of a mess. I picked up her hand. It was quite warm. I thought there might be a dog's chance that she was still alive—just a chance. I opened the crêpe-de-Chinepeignoir she was wearing; put my ear down and listened. There was no result. To make sure I went over to the dressing-table; picked up the hand-mirror, brought it back and tried that. She was dead all right. And she hadn't been dead for long—a matter of minutes, and not too many of them. She had been killed by the woman who'd spoken to me through the door when I'd entered the flat, and that baby had gone out of the door that led to the hall-way—the one on the right; quietly slipped down the stairs and disappeared.

I felt very disappointed, and I didn't like the way things were going. I began to think about Janey. I was disliking Janey more and more every moment.

I went out of the bedroom; started a systematic search of the flat. There was a bathroom and kitchen and a bedroom off the left of the hall door, the sitting-room and the bedroom where I had found the girl. There was nothing. Not that I expected to find anything. The Old Man's agents were too carefully trained not to advertise themselves. There was not even a distinguishing laundry mark on her underthings, and I tell you they were very nice underthings, too. She definitely had taste.

I went into the bathroom, found a soft linen tow-el and came back and spread the towel over the white face and battered head. I sat down on the stool before the dressing-table and looked at what remained of "Madame St. Philippe."

I wondered who she was, what was her real name, and why she was working for the Old Man. I wondered

                                              Peter Cheyney

why in hell a woman with looks, a figure and personali-
ty like this one, should be an agent. I thought life ought
to have found a safer job for her.

Everything about her indicated class. The cut of her
feet and ankles, the well-manicured, long, once-supple
fingers that lay so uselessly beside her.

I thought it was a hell of a waste of woman.

I got up. I said: "O.K., baby. I'll even this up one
day. So long."

I went home.

# II. — THE OLD MAN

**I SAT** back in the driving seat of the Jaguar and relaxed. I was as happy as I ever am. I opened both windows; let the air come into the car.

There isn't any place as comfortable as a car to think in. You can drive mechanically, and just as mechanically you can watch the panorama of the green fields, the trees, villages and the rest of it flash past. If I have to think—and I don't profess to be very fond of the process—I'd rather think in my bath or in the Jaguar than anywhere else.

I put my foot on the accelerator. It was a long, straight road in a fine piece of Berkshire country. I watched the needle go up to seventy; then I checked down to forty; began to think in earnest.

I thought about myself, the Old Man, agents in general and life in particular, which seemed to me to be quite enough to go on with for the moment. First of all I was wondering about what the Old Man's reaction would be to the episode of two days ago in Paris; just what he'd have to say about Madame St. Philippe. Maybe he wouldn't be so pleased about that one. I thought the Old Man might even be quite acid on the whole subject. He was often acid, but out of his acidity and his peculiar frames of mind he produced some extraordinary results. Everybody admitted that— that is if they were still alive to tell the tale after they'd carried out some of his more difficult assignments with the knowledge that if the job wasn't done they would have to undergo the appalling tongue-lashing which the Old Man could produce with extraordinary little effort.

"People put too much value on human life," was one of his favourite remarks. "Everyone has to die sometime—why not now? After all, the world's in a peculiar state and a few days or months or years don't matter all that much. Also there is quite a possibility that the next world might be a darned sight more interesting than this one!"

And no one could accuse him of not having practised what he preached. In his younger days, during the earlier part of World War II, the Old Man had taken every sort of chance in every possible set of circumstances. He was in and out of Germany—very successfully too—five times. He'd been taken by the Gestapo twice and got out of it each time.

He was unique and thought that all his agents ought to be unique, too. If they weren't, they disappeared to lesser organisations or helped run one of his myriad filing systems, with a chip on their shoulder for the rest of their lives.

I thought, quite dispassionately, that agents were odd fish. The fact that I was one myself didn't seem to affect the matter very much. I was taking what I considered to be an objective point of view. Agents—the Old Man's agents—were strange people. Each one of them—man or woman—had different reasons for getting into the oddest of all weird professions. Some of them had drifted into it; some of them had been pushed into it. One of them—a very good one who died in Hungary last year—had been blackmailed into it. I grinned. That was certainly between the devil and the deep sea. But I wondered why a woman like Madame St. Philippe had to be in the business.

Once on a time, one of the cleverest free lance agents that I'd ever met in my life—a man who worked for himself, discovered his own secrets and sold them where he could get most money—told me that the reasons for a man or a woman becoming a secret service agent of any sort, shape or description were exactly the same as the reasons which motivated murder. He said they were greed, jealousy, a desire for revenge or thwarted passion. I remember thinking at the time that he was just nuts. But afterwards experience taught me that there might be a certain amount of sense in what he said.

I looked at my strap-watch. It was ten-past four. Five minutes after that I was driving through Wantage, and then I came on to the straight country road. I slowed down as I approached the first turning to the right; swung the car; found myself in the lane that led up to the wide, white-painted gate. It was a nice spot. I remembered when I had visited it last, a long time ago; it was summer then, and the country smells and flowers were all as ripe as they were now. I stopped the car in front of the gate, got out, pushed the gate open and stood on the lawn that ran round both sides of the house.

It was an attractive house. Really, it was a large cottage with a lawn in front, narrowing as it stretched round the house, broadening at the back. It had a thatched roof. There was a kitchen garden and a flower garden, and a mass of rhododendron bushes towards one side of the house. It looked the sort of place that a retired business man might own. Then the idea of the Old Man as a "retired business man" occurred to me. It made me laugh....

I walked round the right-hand path and rang the front door- bell. The door was opened by a neat maid.

She said: "Mr. Kells? You're expected, Sir. Will you come in?"

I followed her across the hall into the library. She went away and shut the door behind her. I stood just inside the doorway looking at the Old Man. He was sitting in a big chair set beside one of the leaded-paned windows at the end of the room. The window was open, and the sunlight and a little breeze from the flower garden came into the room. I thought the scene looked almost pastoral.

The Old Man sat upright in the chair. God knows how old he is, I don't. But he's been over a lot of grass in his time. His thin face is lined. His deep-set eyes are still of a peculiarly vital blue and he has the largest and bushiest eyebrows I have ever seen. His eyebrows are definitely forbidding. Someone once told me he'd been suffering from a liver disease for the past ten years; that that might be an explanation of his bad temper. But the Old Man has never been particularly bad-tempered with me— only slightly acid.

I said: "Good afternoon. Did you get my message?"

"Of course I did, you damned fool. If I hadn't, you wouldn't have been here now, would you?"

I smiled at him. "Agreed. Let me put it another way.

Did you read my message?"

He said: "Yes, I read it. What's it all about?"

I shrugged my shoulders. "I'm looking for information. Not giving it. You know as much about it as I do."

He brought out a cigarette case and lighted a cigarette. Then he threw the case towards me. I caught it; drew up a chair and sat down opposite him.

I said: "I didn't know there was anything afoot. I was just running the garage and minding my own business. Then the thing happened to Olly. I didn't know whether the man Janey was responsible for it or not. I still don't know. I should think he might be. Then there was the woman. I didn't like that very much."

"No, I don't suppose you would." He went on: "Tell me something, why did you think this woman was working for me?"

That surprised me. "Of course she was working for you. She had the code word Ladies Won't Wait!"

He said: "Does that mean that I gave it to her? There are half a dozen people could have given her it."

"Really?" I raised my eyebrows. "Why?" I asked.

He said: "For God's sake be your age. You know what it's like these days. Our sort of secret service has almost gone to the dogs. In the old days it was a gentleman's profession. Somebody caught an agent on the wrong side of the fence and he disappeared. They just shot him, cut his throat or threw him into a nearby river— something decent like that. Now they don't. They use all sorts of persuasive methods, as you ought to know. The result is that all I can do is to appoint agents for areas just as you're one working in France and Germany.

                    Peter Cheyney

But I don't tell you who you get to work for you. I don't know if you pick a bad one."

I said: "What you're trying to tell me is that this woman wasn't working for you, and that somehow or other she got the code word?"

He said: "That's what I'm telling you. At least that's what I'm telling you at the moment. I might have something different to say later on. I have a dozen women agents working in Europe, and they don't telephone through every morning to say that they're still alive. Maybe something will turn up eventually, but at the moment I don't know anything about your Madame St. Philippe."

I said: "That's damned funny. She was English, and she was a remarkably beautiful woman."

"Many female agents are beautiful," said the Old Man. "In some cases that's their only qualification for the job."

I said: "This makes it very interesting—very interesting indeed. I wonder what it was she was trying to tell me."

The Old Man said: "How the devil would I know? And who said she was going to tell you something? Maybe she wanted to get something out of you. Having got that code word maybe she thought you'd trust her." He grinned cynically.

"Like hell...!" I said. "You've known me too long to think I belong to the trusting type."

He grunted. "I must say you've been pretty hard-boiled."

There was silence for a moment. I thought the Old

Man was being very argumentative.

I said: "Well, the general idea is that I want to know whether I go back and go on running the garage until I hear from you, or whether I try to do something about this."

He shrugged his shoulders. "There's no harm in you trying, Kells." He stubbed out his cigarette. "You know all this thing stems from Rockie."

I said: "I gathered that."

The Old Man got up. He began to walk about the room. I noticed with admiration the straightness of his back, the set of his shoulders. I thought some time—a long time ago—the Old Man had been a soldier, and I bet he was a good one, too.

He said: "The whole thing stems from Rockie. I sent Rockie into Germany a year ago on both sides of the line. He did very well. Anybody who says you can't bribe the Russians ought to have seen Rockie at work. He was just as welcome in their zone as he was in ours. He was pretty good. He had a lot of money of his own and he regarded his job with us as a sort of sport. He was the mouse who liked to put his head in the lion's mouth just to see if one day the lion would get angry and bite it off. Well, it looks to me as if the lion got angry."

I asked: "Did they get him?"

He shrugged his shoulders. "I suppose so. He disappeared. He disappeared about four months ago, since when nobody has heard anything of him at all. I put out the usual feelers and tipped off such agents as I could get at who were working in the area to try and get a line on what had happened to him. But up to now nothing has come to light."

I said: "Well, that's just another agent who's disappeared, that's all."

He grunted again. "I don't mind agents disappearing. I don't like it, especially if they're good ones, but I don't mind it if it's been worth while. After all——" he looked at me sideways— "you've got to regard agents as being expendable people. You've got to be prepared for them to disappear or be found in a gutter somewhere with their necks broken or something like that. You know that."

I nodded.

"The devil of it was," the Old Man went on, "that Rockie was on to something. I told you he disappeared about four months ago. Two or three weeks before that he got a message back to me. He was on to something pretty big. He didn't indicate what it was, but he did indicate that it was necessary that he talked to me about it. It was too big to commit to any messenger or telephone or post. He wanted to see me."

I asked: "Have you any ideas as to what was in his mind?"

"No, I haven't the remotest idea. It may have been a lot of things. It might have been Korea. That broke soon after I heard from him. It might have been something even more important than that."

"What was he doing, and where was he when he disappeared?" I asked.

He said: "You ought to know. You were up there. You saw him several times. He was in Frankfurt. He was supposed to be playing around there having a good time. He had his sister with him."

I said: "She was the woman whom Janey told me about—the beautiful sister. Is she beautiful?"

The Old Man said: "I think she's a knock-out from what I've heard."

I asked: "Did she know anything about Rockie? Did she know that he worked for you?"

"I don't know. If she did the only person who'd have told her would have been Rockie. I can't see him telling anybody except under duress."

"What do you mean by that?" I asked.

He said: "Well, if Rockie was in a hell of a spot; if he'd thought that they were going to knock him off or grab him, or do whatever they've done, he might have talked to his sister. He'd trust her. He'd know, or he'd hope, that she wouldn't let him down."

I asked: "Have you seen her?"

He shook his head. "Why should I? She came back to England via France about two weeks after Rockie disappeared. When he didn't turn up at the hotel she raised a terrific commotion. All the hospitals were searched—the usual thing. Military Intelligence came into it and tried to discover if Rockie had been playing around in the Russian zone or somewhere. They got damned little help from the Russians. Maybe he's in a concentration camp." He grinned. "I can't see Rockie in a concentration camp, any more than I could see you in one. I should think he'd make himself so damned objectionable that the least they could do would be to kill him."

I said: "The sister made no attempt to get into touch

                                          Peter Cheyney

with you or see you?"

He shook his head.

"Then," I said, "it's a stone certainty Rockie said nothing to her. If he'd told her what he was doing, or made any sort of suggestion about being in danger, he'd have told her your name and she'd have tried to get in touch with you."

He nodded. "That's what I thought. She hasn't tried to get in touch with me, so I imagine she knows nothing."

I said: "I want to come back to Madame St. Philippe. She rather upsets things a little, doesn't she?"

"How does she upset things?" he asked.

"Work it out for yourself," I said. "If Madame St. Philippe were working for you, or for one of your people, even if you knew nothing about her, it would be obvious for her to try and get in touch with me. If somebody on the other side, somebody who knew about the Rockie affair, connected her with that, it would be quite on the cards that they would want to kill her before she got a chance to talk to me, and it would be all very reasonable and logical if she were working for you. But she's not working for you, so why was she killed?"

The Old Man said: "I don't know. I could make a couple of guesses." He grinned at me rather unpleasantly.

"All right," I said. "Make a couple of guesses for my benefit."

He said: "Look, this woman, who is beautiful and well-dressed and glamorous, picks you up in the street in Paris. She gives you the code word of the month. She wants to talk to you. The business is so urgent and so very important that she wouldn't write to you or talk to you on the telephone, or go round to your apartment. Damn it, she could have gone to see you at the garage. But no, it's all much too important for that. You have to see her at this address. And you walk round there because you're too clever even to take a taxicab, and when you get there someone's just about to kill her, or has killed her. And this somebody disappears very quietly—so quickly and quietly that you don't even get a look at her. And you're left holding the baby."

I said: "I see...."

"Precisely," said the Old Man. "Maybe it was intended that you should be discovered with the dead woman. Perhaps the idea was to have you run in on a murder charge. Maybe the plan went wrong and whoever it was was intended to turn up and catch you with this unfortunate, battered female didn't do it, which was very lucky for you. By the way, did you find anything that was used on the dead woman—a spanner or a club or anything?"

I said: "No, there was nothing. It had been taken away."

"Exactly," said the Old Man. "If somebody was trying to frame you, obviously they'd take the murder weapon away. It would have had fingerprints on it. That would be all right. If you were caught with the body you might have got rid of the weapon, concealed it or something. But," he went on, "all this is guessing, isn't it?"

I said: "Yes. It all seems very unsatisfactory to me, except that I'm rather pleased at not having been discovered with the once beautiful corpse."

                                    Peter Cheyney

"Maybe," he said. "But somebody may know about it. They may still try to do a little blackmail." He grinned again. He went on: "I said 'try' I should hate to blackmail you, Kells."

I said: "It's been tried before like everything else. Well, what am I supposed to do about all this?"

He said: "I don't mind. Rockie was rather a friend of yours, wasn't he? It might be interesting to discover what it was he'd found out; what it was he wanted to see me about. It might be interesting to discover what happened to him if such a process is possible." He looked at me wryly. "Perhaps you might like to find those things out in your odd moments."

I grinned at him. "All right. Is there anything else?"

He said: "No. You do what you like. You can go back to Paris or you can go to Frankfurt, or you can stay here. If you don't find somebody out, I think you'll find somebody will find you out."

"Meaning what?" I asked.

He said: "My dear feller, whoever it was put that woman on to you is not going to rest content with the situation. They're going to do something else, aren't they?"

I said: "I suppose so."

The Old Man looked at his watch. "I have an appointment in twenty minutes, and I don't want you here. You'll find a bottle of whisky next door in the dining-room. Have a drink and get away from here, will you? And good luck to you, Kells."

I said: "Thanks a lot. I've an idea I'm going to need it."

He said, airily: "You never know. You're all right about drawing money and things like that, aren't you?"

"Oh, yes, that part's all right."

"Well, be careful," said the Old Man. "I should hate to have to try to replace you. I think that once or twice since you've been working for me you've been very good."

I said: "I'd like to tell you exactly what I think about you, except I can't think of enough really strong language. So long!"

I went out, had the whisky and soda in the dining-room. Then I drove back to London. I went back on a different road from the one I'd come on.

**WHEN** I woke up next morning the sun was shining. I yawned; got out of bed; began to walk about my bedroom and drawing-room in my bare feet, rather enjoying the sensation. I had an apartment in Knightsbridge—one of a dozen which were kept specially for the use of people like me who were working for the Old Man. I rang down for coffee, lighted a cigarette and tried to do a little straight thinking.

One of the disadvantages of my sort of job is that you never really know what you're doing, and if the Old Man is ever good enough to give an indication it is usually so vague it doesn't mean anything at all. Which, when you come to think of it, is rather clever on his part. Running a job like his must be hell. Especially when you realise exactly what he was up against. He just couldn't trust an agent all the way, not because he didn't want to trust him but because the more definite the information in the possession of the agent the more the other side could get out of him, by some means or other. The Old Man knew just as well as you or I know that everyone has a breaking point and there are all sorts of clever processes by which the toughest egg can be made to talk—even if he really doesn't want to and is trying hard not to. Now they've got a new one—the "sleep treatment" under which a man can be persuaded to open up and talk whilst he's asleep and, when he wakes up, knows nothing about it.

Then there was another angle. The Old Man might, for all I knew, know plenty more about the Rockie business, but it just didn't suit his book at the moment to tell me. Firstly, because they might get me and try to make me talk... I said try... and, secondly, because it was on the cards that he had three or four other people on this job, each working in a different sector, and the Old Man would, from time to time, pass on to the agents concerned scraps of information that might assist them in their part of the job.

But the Old Man's general technique is very simple. The idea is that if sufficient agents get themselves into sufficient trouble in sufficient places something quite tangible is going to emerge, and when it does emerge he can do something about it. In the meantime one feels about in the dark, probing for tender places in the enemy's line, supposing you know who the enemy is and if he's got a line.

I thought about my conversation with him. I could develop an active or a passive frame of mind about this Rockie business. If I wanted to be active I could go back to Frankfurt, try and dig up some of Rockie's old connections there, do a little travelling, call a great deal of attention to myself and probably get knocked off by some enterprising Russian in the Soviet Sector for sticking my neck out, and once those boys do get you it's a toss up whether you ever come back or not. You might even find yourself working in a salt mine or something.

That was one active angle. The second one was I could go and see Rockie's sister—this beautiful and alluring lady I'd heard so much about. Just at the moment it seemed commonsense not to do that. If she'd known what Rockie was doing; if she'd had any idea what had happened to him, she'd have talked to somebody about it. If Rockie had told her about the sort of work he was really doing she'd have had enough sense to have got into touch with one of the M.I. Departments—M.I.5 or some of those boys.

But my guess was that Rockie talked to nobody; that he hadn't talked to her. And I was basing my guess on my knowledge of Rockie. That boy was as tough as hell and as hard as nails, and he trusted nobody outside the very small group with which he was working. He certainly wasn't the sort of person who'd trust his own sister with a hell of a big story merely because she washis sister.

But of course you never knew. When a man's an extremist he'd do all sorts of things—even Rockie. Just for the moment I played with the idea that she might know something about it, and for reasons best known to herself she had kept her information to herself. I didn't see why she should have done that, but supposing she

                                    Peter Cheyney

had. Why would she behave like that? I shrugged my shoulders. There certainly wasn't any answer to that one at the moment. Also, in any event, it didn't matter all that just at this time. Maybe, sometime or other, I'd get around to taking a long look at Rockie's sister even if only to satisfy my curiosity about the woman that Janey thought was such a marvellous person.

I came back to the passive angles. I could just sit quietly where I was and do nothing about it (except possibly take a week-end now and again in Paris to see how the garage was going), and wait for something to happen. The Old Man's theory was that whoever it was had tried to contact me through the charming Madame St. Philippe would want to do it again. I was intrigued of course because the Old Man said he didn't know anything about her. I knew perfectly well that no responsible agent was going to give a woman about whom he knew little the code word, and get her to contact me, unless he was in a pretty bad way or unless the situation was fairly desperate. That might have happened, but I was disinclined to believe it.

On the other hand somebody might have put her in just to make a mess of things for me by telling me some odd story that had been concocted, or getting me off to some place. But I wondered why they should be particularly interested in me at the moment. I hadn't even been doing anything relatively important. I wasn't actually working on any particular angle for the Old Man. I was simply in the position of being his chief field agent in Paris, waiting there, ostensibly running my garage, until something broke and he needed me.

You never knew with women. For two very good reasons. One, women always manage to start something if they're good-looking and attractive—even if they are on your side. The second thing is that immediately women arrive on the scene everyone begins to use their imagination like hell and very often creates the most alarming situations out of nothing.

I remember one time I was working in Poland with a man who was doing an important job for the Old Man. This man—his name was Clissel; he's dead now—was to await the arrival of an Englishwoman who was to give him certain carefully concealed information. Eventually, she arrived and it was only five days afterwards that Clissel realised that, so far as he was concerned, she was the wrong woman! She was just a distant relative he hadn't seen for years. She'd recognised him and started a conversation with him to satisfy herself that he washer relative.

And she was damned difficult to get rid of. Clissel passed her on to me, and it took four hard days' work to persuade her to get out of Danzig before fur began to fly.

But at the back of my mind was the definite idea that the appearance of the alluring Madame St. Philippe, my rather peculiar meeting with Janey who said he'd got my address at The Travellers' Club and hadn't, my just as sudden meeting with Marcini, all on the same day, finishing up with the murder of the woman, for some reason which I could not determine, tied the whole thing in with Rockie. I was certain it all had something to do with Rockie. I remembered what Janey had said

                                    Peter Cheyney

about Rockie's sister, about her living in Sussex; about my going down there to see her. It looked as if he was rather wanting me to do that. I shrugged my shoulders. Maybe, when the time came, we'd try it on.

At eleven o'clock I stopped pondering on these weighty matters; bathed, shaved, dressed myself carefully and went down to the watchmaker's shop near St. John's Gate. It was open. In the little compartment at the end of the long counter, with the watchmaker's glass screwed into his eye, was Silenski. Silenski is interesting enough for me to tell you a little about him.

He'd been working for the Old Man since the Germans went into Poland, and he had had some of the most extraordinary things happen to him. Some Poles are very tough, but I've never known anybody as tough as Silenski. He'd only one eye—somebody had put the other one out. He was burned all over. But he was a fellow who'd never had enough. He was always prepared to have another go when it was desired of him. Actually, the Old Man, who I suppose had some sort of sympathy deep down in the bottom of his acid stomach, had kept him in London for quite a time. Silenski ran the watchmaker's shop near St. John's Gate and acted as a sort of general liaison for anyone who was operating in London. I thought he might be useful to me.

I went into the shop, walked along the counter, put my head in his cubby-hole, and said in Polish: "Well, how's it going, Silenski?"

He looked up at me. He said: "For crying out loud... Mike... ! So you're still alive?"

I said: "It looks like it."

"Everything is very quiet," said Silenski. "I sit here and I repair watches. I've seen one or two of the boys—Grigor, who is a Pole and whom I think you know. He was here three weeks ago. Then he went away and has disappeared. Rosanski, the White Russian, whom you also know, is dead." He grinned. "Everybody seems to be dying before their time." He shrugged his shoulders. "If they wait a little while, in a minute there will be a nice fat war. Then everybody can die. The things that are going on..." Silenski continued, "I promise you, Michael, that nobody would believe them."

I nodded. What he said was, of course, quite true. Nobody does believe them. And people are not curious any more. I suppose they're too busy minding their own business and trying to solve their own problems to worry too much about satisfying their curiosity. Or maybe they read too many detective stories to believe in anything at all.

To-day the strangest things happen everywhere—including England. But nobody worries. Events pose the most amazing questions but nobody takes any notice.

I remember when I was crossing from France on the Invictasomeone lent me a copy of an English newspaper. I read an extraordinary story (maybe you read it too) of an old man who kept a sweet shop in some little village in England, who had been murdered, quite obviously not for gain, because there was quite a little money in the till which the murderer had not touched. The police wished to question two men about it. They got one man who didn't want to talk, so they went after the second man. This boyo, through the services of a foreign embassy in London, had managed to get himself smuggled aboard a ship. When the ship was stopped at sea by the British authorities, the Captain—who was a foreigner—refused to give the man up although he didn't refuse to give him up when the ship was stopped a day or two later by a Russian tug. The Russians took the man away and that was that. A nice story with interesting implications. Except that nobody seemed to bother sufficiently to find out what they were.

I said to Silenski: "How's the girl friend?"

He smiled. "Carla is very well. Don't you want to talk to her? She's upstairs."

I said: "I'll go and talk to her."

I went through the little room at the back of the shop and up the stairs. At the top of the stairs was a sitting-room. A cosy, comfortably furnished room with flowers tastefully arranged. Carla was sitting in an armchair reading The Tatler.

I tell you she was something. She was one of those women at whom you take a quick glance and then look again just to make certain that you aren't dreaming. She was a Pole, and when Polish women are beautiful they really are, if you know what I mean. She was Polish and passionate and lush. When she looked at you there was that indefinable question in her eyes.

Carla exuded passion like a bottle of Chanel No. 5 exudes perfume. She was as cool as cucumber, as wicked (if need be) as a snake and filled with the most extraordinary conglomeration of complexes where men were concerned. With control she was the ideal woman agent. I said with control. Without it she was just another lovely sick headache.

I can only explain what I mean by trying to give an example. Thus, supposing Silenski wanted to obtain some information about another Pole in the old days he used to put Carla on to the man's best friend. Carla would start by falling in love with this man or at least giving a very good impression of it, and she would put everything she knew into the business of adoring this individual until she had found out what she wanted; then she'd press another button and become entirely disinterested in him. A very good type of woman agent to have working with you, but not very good to have against you.

She was tall, curved in all the right places, looked very well in her clothes. She had jet black hair, and peculiarly luminous eyes of an odd amethyst colour. Actually, I was never quite certain what colour her eyes were. She spoke four languages perfectly, and reserved her Polish accent when speaking English only for somebody whom she wished to impress.

She got up from the chair quickly and gracefully. She threw her arms round my neck and kissed me on the mouth and when I say kissed I mean kissed.

She said: "Michael, this is like all my old dreams coming true. Life has been for me a desert until to-day. Now I see you and I am happy."

I said: "Look, how do you think this would go with Silenski— the one downstairs who is playing with the innards of a watch?"

She stood away from me. She looked at me hard. She said: "Michael, you should know that Silenski understands me. He knows my strange nature. He knows that quite a lot of the time I think about him and all the rest of the time I only think about you."

I grinned. "Of course. And who else?"

"Nobody else," she said. "What are you doing here?"

"Nothing particularly. Just hanging around. But I thought I'd come down in case I needed a little assistance during the next week or so. From you or Silenski or anyone else you've got on the books in London and not working. Anybody I know?"

She nodded. "There's Mrs. Vayne. She's not doing anything, and she's living in Kensington. And there's that nice man from Devonshire—the one with the accent—Glyder. You know, the one with the finger missing from his left hand. And there's the young man who was in the Brigade of Guards—Terence Maydew."

I said: "A nice selection—Mrs. Vayne—fair, fat and forty, Maydew, who's not awfully experienced, and Glyder, who certainly is. Besides which there's Silenski, myself and"—I laughed at her—"if things become very serious—you."

She said: "Of course, Michael. You know perfectly well that for you I'd lay myself down under a tram."

"That's nice of you, but I don't see it'd do me any good." I picked up my hat. "Well, it's been nice seeing you, Carla. Write down your telephone number for me."

She wrote it down. She said: "There's always somebody here— someone you can trust—either Mrs. Vayne or Silenski or myself. There's always someone to answer the telephone."

I asked: "When did Silenski see the Old Man last?"

"He hasn't seen him. He heard from him yesterday on the telephone. He said he thought you might be calling in. Did you know he'd telephoned?"

I shook my head. "No. He must be a mind-reader. So long, Carla."

I picked up the piece of paper with the telephone number on it; went downstairs.

I said so long to Silenski. He took the jeweller's glass out of his eye. He said: "You saw Carla?"

I said: "Yes, she's looking very well."

"That's what I thought," said Silenski. "I don't like the new lipstick she's wearing, and there's a lot of it on your face. So long, Mike."

I wiped the lipstick off my mouth and went out.

**I SPENT** most of the day hanging around. I had lunch and tea, went into the club for a drink, read the newspapers. I was quite happy. I've always found it's a good thing not to be in too much of a hurry about anything, never to be afraid of marking time for a bit. Also at the back of my head I had an idea something would happen fairly soon. I've always found if you wait for something to happen it always does. It happened all right.

I went home about half-past seven. My idea was to change my clothes, drink another cocktail, have dinner somewhere and go to bed and sleep the sleep of the just. This seemed a fairly good idea.

When I got to the flat I opened the door and saw the invitation card. It had been pushed under the crack of the door and lay there looking up at me. I picked it up. It was a nice card with a gilt edge and of an exotic pinkish colour with violet lettering on it, and it said that Madame Olga Volanski—Haute Couture, Furs and Model Gowns—would be honoured by my presence at her cocktail party at 23 Crestwick Court, St. John's Wood. The card was perfumed. The perfume was very nice. I wondered who Madame Volanski was. I thought I bet she's a good one. I was very glad she hoped to be honoured with my presence. Anyway, she was pretty well covered. The card was one of those things giving people invitations to dress shows or parties connected with dress. It was perfectly simple for one of them to have got under the wrong door. I knew that delivery agencies were often employed to deliver such invitations almost promiscuously.

But I didn't think it was a mistake. I thought that Madame Volanski might be very interested in me.

I thought we might have a lot to say to each other.

# III. — CARLA

**I ARRIVED** at Crestwick Court in St. John's Wood soon after nine. I stopped the cab fifty or sixty yards from the apartment block, paid off the driver and walked slowly towards the tube station. Half way there, was the car. Inside was Carla.

I helped her out. I said: "Carla, you look wonderful!"

And she did. She was wearing a close-fitting, superbly cut, gold lamé dinner frock, and over it a long, black velvet cloak, caught at the neck with a gold chain. Her sandals were gold and with the highest heels I've ever seen, but they suited her. She looked good enough to eat.

She said: "When you telephoned I spent some time asking myself what I was to wear. I wished to look my best for you. After I saw you earlier to-day I began to think about you. I thought about you passionately... but quite vehemently. I realised that never in my life... no matter how sincere I may have thought myself to have been at the time... never have I loved any man as I love you. Embrace me!"

"Like hell," I said. "This is no time for embraces. There's a little work to be done."

She said: "Mike, what's going on? Tell me, does something exciting happen?"

I shrugged my shoulders. "I don't know. We're going to a cocktail party given by a Madame Volanski. When I arrived back this evening I found the invitation card pushed under my door."

She nodded. "What do you want me to do?"

I said: "I don't know. This cocktail party might be one of those things, but on the other hand it might be something else. But, in any event, I thought I'd like to have you with me."

Madame Volanski's flat was on the second floor at Crestwick Court—a large and, I should imagine, expensive block of apartments, and her party was, I think, the most alarming one I've ever seen. I'd hardly got my finger on the bell-push before the door was opened by an individual who, I found later, was the butler. He was dressed in black evening dress trousers; a white serge tuxedo. He had a bloated, evil face. He smelled strongly of gin.

The hallway was large, and on the other side of it the double doors leading to the drawing-room were wide open. The room was crammed with some of the most extraordinary people. It was just impossible to place them. They were tall and short, and fat and thin—Englishmen and foreigners. Some of the women wore expensive evening frocks; some coats and skirts; some a strange collection of clothes which looked as if they had been hired from a dress agency.

Whilst the butler was taking our things, a woman came out of the drawing-room; crossed the hall. I had to look at her twice before I could make myself believe it was true.

She was a large strawberry blonde, and she was wearing a black and white striped evening frock that seemed much too tight for her in all the wrong places. Her face was large, and her complexion might have been good, but her features were so caked with impossible make-up that the colour of the skin underneath was not distinguishable. Her mouth was painted in a bright scarlet cupid's bow. I thought she looked awful.

She came over to us, one plump hand, loaded with rings, outstretched.

She said with a Russian accent: "I am so glad to see you, I am Madame Volanski. Welcome to my party."

I said: "It was very nice of you to ask me, Madame. I wonder why you did. My name's Kells. This is Madame Carla, my cousin. I brought her because she is thinking of opening a dress shop. I thought you might have a wrinkle or two for her."

"But of course..." She shrugged her shoulders. "But, you see, you 'ave come too late. There was a dress show at 'alf past six. Now it ees all over. People are just talking, 'aving a dreenk and being 'appy."

I looked at the people who were being happy. A man disengaged himself from the crowd; moved rapidly through the door; ran down the corridor in the direction of the bathroom. Either Madame's liquor or his stomach had gone back on him.

She said: "You will forgive me if I say that your cousin is ver' beautiful. I appreciate beauty in all its forms."

I said: "I am very glad to hear it."

She led the way into the drawing-room.

She said: "Meester Kells, I theenk you are going to like my brother so I am going to find 'eem for you, and you two can 'ave some dreenks together and I will talk to your cousin, Madame Carla."

                    

I said: "It's very kind of you."

"Not at all. You wait for me 'ere." She went away.

Carla said: "I think this is going to be rather amusing. I think that woman is a goddam phoney."

I agreed with her.

Madame Volanski returned. Behind her, over-shadowing her with his bulk, was an immense man. He was about six feet three in height, of huge proportions. His face was large and round. His hair was black and curly. He had an immense cavalry moustache. He was wearing evening tails, with a ribbon in his button-hole.

He put out his hand. He said in a gruff voice: "I am delighted to meet you." He bent low over Carla's hand. "Madame Carla, it gives me the greatest pleasure to make your acquaintance. I think you are a mos' lovely woman." He turned to me. "But I must tear myself away from the beautiful Madame Carla so that I may talk to you, M'sieu Kells. Per'aps we have met somewhere before? Per'aps you have been to Russia in the old days?"

I said: "No, I haven't been to Russia in the old days. Was it nice?"

"You don' know anything about life if you don' know those days in Russia. Come with me."

We moved across the drawing-room, Madame Volanski's brother pushing ahead of me, moving people out of the way with immense, spatulate-fingered hands. On the other side of the drawing-room was a passage; at the end of this was a small room. It was filled with bottles and glasses, evidently used as a reserve store-room for the festivities outside.

He asked: "What would you like to drink? If you like, I will give you some vodka—real vodka. I tell you there is nothing like it."

I said: "All right, I'll drink vodka."

He opened a bottle: poured out two glasses. I should think there was nearly a quarter of a pint of liquor in each glass. He put the glass to his mouth, threw back his head and the vodka was gone.

He said: "That is the only way to drink vodka."

"It's nice to watch you," I said, "but if you don't mind, I'll just sip mine." I sat down.

He put his great bulk on to the table; refilled his glass; sat there looking at me. He said: "You interest me ver' much, M'sieu Kells. You must understand that my name is Alexis Alexandrov. I was Hetman of Cossacks in Korniloff's army in 1918."

I raised my eyebrows. "No? You must have been awfully young to have been Hetman of Cossacks in 1918."

He smiled. "I was awfully young, but still I was Hetman of Cossacks at seventeen years of age. I had killed men when I was sixteen."

I nodded. "I'd rather be on your side."

There was a pause. He produced a gold cigarette case; selected a cigarette; handed the case to me. The cigarettes were Russian— rather sweet and a little sickly in taste.

He said: "I am interested in you, M'sieu Kells, because you look to me like a man of the world. I am interested to know what you think of this peculiar world of ours. Do you think it is a nice place to live in?"

I shrugged my shoulders. "That rather depends on

  

point of view, doesn't it. I see nothing the matter with the world as a world. It's simply that the people in it don't seem to be getting along very well together."

He said: "What you have to understand, M'sieu Kells, is that there is not going to be any peace in the world until somebody decides what is going to be done with Russia. Don' you understand this?"

"Yes... possibly... But who is going to decide what is to be done with Russia?"

He said: "Somebody's got to. And per'aps it will be the Russians who will decide."

I said: "Maybe. What do you think they'll decide to do? I don't think Russia wants to fight anybody any more than any other nation in the world."

"Per'aps you are right," said Alexandrov. "Per'aps in a minute she will decide to fight herself. That is what I hope."

"You don't mean to say you consider there's a possibility of a revolution in Russia?"

He looked at me with wide eyes. Beneath his black moustaches his teeth glistened. "And why not? Everybody is so very funny about that. Why should not there be a revolution? The Russians are always revolting against something. They are born revolutionists. It is a sort of habit with them, you know."

I nodded. "I suppose if there were a revolution you'd go back, Alexandrov?"

He said: "Of course..." He got up from the table; expanded his chest. "I shall go back and fight. I love fighting. It is a marvellous sport."

I finished my drink.

He said: "M'sieu Kells, if you wish to be alone, you stay here and have some drinks. If you wish to be with other people go back to the drawing-room. Most of them are friends of Madame Volanski, my sister. Most of them are what you call bloody fools. But for me I must leave you. I must leave you because I must go and find your lovely cousin. I want to talk to her. You know, directly she came into this apartment I looked at her and said: 'This woman is lovely and she is a Pole.'"

I said: "You're perfectly right on both counts. She is a Pole."

"She looks to me very intelligent," said Alexandrov. "When I meet beauty in a woman I am delighted. And when also she is intelligent then I am enchanted. For the moment, au revoir...."

He went out of the room.

I walked round the room searching amongst the large collection of bottles until I found some whisky. I found a siphon and a clean glass; poured myself a drink; sat down again. I began to think about Madame Volanski and her effusive brother, the late Hetman of Cossacks. I thought they were an interesting pair. And perhaps not so interesting as odd. I thought Carla had been right about Madame Volanski. She was a phoney. Everything about her exuded spuriousness in a big way. Quite obviously the invitation I had received was a plant. For some reason or other these people wanted me to come to their party, and I supposed the reason would emerge a little later on.

And I didn't go for Alexandrov. Not at all. His Russian accent—and I speak the language—was rather peculiar, and I thought the Hetman of Cossacks stuff was just bunk. It occurred to me that there was something almost amateurish about the pair of them, rather as if they'd taken on something that was a little too big for them and realised it before they'd started on the job.

After a few minutes I walked back into the drawing-room. The party had thinned out. There were still little groups of people talking quietly or arguing in corners. There were one or two glassy-eyed ladies of uncertain ages who walked from group to group with the peculiar expression of the unsatisfied and slighted virgin in search of prey.

But the sting had gone out of the party. I walked across the drawing-room, through the door on the other side—the doorway that led away from the hallway—into a corridor. At the end of the corridor a door leading into a lighted room was half open. I put my head round it.

Madame Volanski was sitting in a high-backed chair in front of an old refectory table. She had a bottle and a large glass of vodka in her hand. She was sipping the vodka and crying into the glass.

I looked round the room. It had the appearance of a library. There were bookshelves filled with volumes. It also had the appearance of being used more than the other rooms in the apartment. I went in. I stood on the other side of the table looking at her.

I asked: "Is anything wrong? Can I help?"

"No, Meester Kells. You cannot do anything. You see, I live in a sort of vicious circle. When I am sober I am so un'appy I cry. When I cry Alexis says to me 'For

God's sake stop crying, you drive me mad,' so to stop crying I dreenk some vodka. And when I dreenk vodka I cry, because vodka makes me cry. So you see, Meester Kells, there ees not a great deal of 'ope for me to stop crying."

I asked: "Have you ever tried eating, as apart from drinking I mean?"

She shook her head. "Who wants to eat? I don' want to eat. I am too miserable. I wish only to die."

I walked back to the door and shut it. I returned; drew up a chair; sat down facing her across the table.

She said: "Would you like a dreenk?" She pushed the bottle across to me.

I said: "Not for the moment. I feel very sorry for you. I suppose all White Russians are inclined to be unhappy?"

She nodded. "I think all Russians are un'appy, but especially the White Russians. For them there ees no 'ope at all... not for people like Alexis."

I asked: "Why is it worse for Alexis? He seems to me to be a very cheerful sort of fellow. A large, experienced man of the world who loves fighting, drinking and loving, and who probably is feeling slightly frustrated at the moment because he isn't getting enough of these things—except possibly, drinking."

"Per'aps," she said. "But Alexis ees a fool. Always 'e picks the wrong people. Especially the women. Always they are winding 'eem round their fingers..."

I thought she was pulling a line and doing it rather badly. She was using the oldest trick in the world. Trying to belittle Alexandrov; to make him out a fool.

                    Peter Cheyney

I thought that he might be a fool, but not that sort of fool.

I said: "I would never have thought that Alexis would have trouble with women. Maybe he's too attractive."

She shrugged her shoulders. She made a deprecatory gesture with her hands. She said: "Alexis...! All my life I have spent trying to get Alexis out of trouble. You understand? 'E ees always getting 'eemself into trouble."

I asked: "Why?"

She shrugged again. "It ees the wrong sort of people 'e mixes with. Wherever you find Alexis you find a lot of no-goods about 'eem. Sometimes it does not matter because it ees children's stuff... you know, like playing the Robin 'ood or Dick Turpin. These people do not matter. But sometimes it ees not peoples like that. Sometimes it ees people like those 'e ees mixed up with now. They are not good."

I said: "Who are they? I think it is very interesting. I think something should be done to save Alexis from himself. Who are these people?"

She looked at me sideways. I thought that at some time or other she had been quite attractive. I wondered what the hell she was playing at.

She said: "I don' know. But I would like to know. That ees what I would like to do. You see, Alexis 'as been in troubles all 'is life. I want that to stop. I don' want 'eem to be mixed up with strange peoples any more. First of all a long time ago we got out of Russia; then we got out of Poland; then we got out of a lot of other countries. Then we go to France."

I asked: "Did Alexis get into trouble in France?"

She nodded. She spread her hands. "But, of course...! So we are asked to leave France if we don' mind. It was not anything ver' much, you understand. Alexis got mixed up in some ver' big card game. Some American lost a great deal of money. That would not have mattered per'aps, but 'e was attached to the American Embassy. So the Préfecture of Police thought it might be a good idea if Alexis went away.

"So we came 'ere. I start this dress business, and I am doing ver' well. Always I can make some monies. But I cannot make myself any 'appiness."

I said: "And do you think Alexis is up to something?"

She nodded. "I don' theenk anything about it, Meester Kells. I know 'e ees." She sighed. She refilled her glass; drank some more vodka. The tears were running down each side of her nose. She looked like a pathetic comedienne.

She went on: "I don' know why I am talking to you like thees, except that I theenk you are a nice man. You look as if you are 'uman and 'ave understanding."

I said: "That's very nice of you, Madame Volanski."

She put her hand across the table; it rested on mine. It was a plump, white hand. There was a diamond ring on the second finger which must have cost a lot of money.

She said: "Don' call me Madame Volanski. Call me Olga."

"I think Olga is a lovely name," I said. "Tell me something, Olga, why did you invite me to this party? Was my name on a list of yours, or did you just get an idea?"



Peter Cheyney

She shrugged her shoulders. "I don' know. You see, I 'ave these parties. I ask so many of my friends. And then I go to an agency to ask other important peoples in London who are interested in frocks to come. So quite often there are lots of peoples at my parties whom I do not know. It does not matter. It ees good for business. I have met people with whom I 'ave done a lot of business like that. It was probably the agency who ask you."

I said: "Well, I'm glad they did because I'm having a very enjoyable time."

There was a silence; then she said: "You know, Meester Kells, one morning I would like to 'ave a talk with you. One morning I would like to meet you somewhere where there ees not any vodka. Per'aps we could 'ave lunch together. Per'aps we could 'ave a talk. Per'aps I could tell you some things that would interest you a lot." She looked at me. Her eyes were filled with tears. But they still looked very interesting, very intriguing. I thought that Olga Volanski was definitely a character.

I said: "That's an idea. Give me your telephone number. I'll ring you."

She said: "I will give you a card. When you think you would like to talk to me; when you think the time 'as come when you would like to invite me to lunch, ring me up."

"I will, Olga," I said. "And sooner than you think." I got up; put the card in my pocket. "Well, I'll be seeing you!"

She said: "Yes... I 'ave no doubt... Fate 'as said our paths shall cross." She drank some more vodka.

I went back to the drawing-room. There were only

about ten people there. I remembered the whisky. I walked across the room to the little store where I'd talked with Alexandrov. The room was dark. I switched on the electric light by the doorway; stood looking into the room.

On the other side of the room behind the table, Carla was enveloped in the arms of the ex-Hetman of Cossacks. They were in the middle of a passionate embrace.

I said: "Don't let me interrupt anything."

Alexandrov released Carla. She stood, gasping a little, re- adjusting her hair.

She said: "You know, Michael, this man Alexis is like a bear— a Russian bear. But I find him very interesting."

Alexandrov said: "I am a very interesting man. Always I do everything better than any other man. I am bigger. I am more handsome. I fight better and I make love in the most amazing way." He indicated Carla. "This woman has fallen for me in a big way, M'sieu Kells. I think I shall probably marry her sometime." He moved to the table; poured himself a drink.

Carla gave me a very quick wink. I nodded my head.

I said: "I've been trying to find you, Alexandrov. I wanted to say good night to you. I'm on my way." I turned to Carla. "Would you like to come back, my dear, or shall Alexandrov bring you back?"

She said: "I'll stay for a little while—just a little while. Must you go?"

"Yes, I've an appointment. But I shall be free in about half an hour's time. Shall I come back for you?"

She shook her head. "No, Michael... to-night I

                                    Peter Cheyney

can look after myself." She threw a love-lorn glance at Alexandrov.

He said: "Kells... you will not worry about Carla. I wish to talk to her. When she wishes to go away I shall look after her. Good night to you."

"All right," I said. "Good night to you." I winked surreptitiously at Carla. "Don't do anything I wouldn't like to read about in the papers."

I went back into the drawing-room; crossed it; walked along the passageway and took a final peep at Olga. She was sitting where I had left her, looking at the half-filled glass of vodka, her eyes pouring with tears. She didn't see me. I went back into the drawing-room, crossed the hallway, took my hat, opened the door and went out. I thought it had been a very interesting party.

Outside, it was a fine night with a moon and a gentle breeze. I began to walk back to my apartment.

I thought that there hadn't been any "mistake" in the invitation to the Volanski party being left at my flat. Somebody, either Olga Volanski or her brother, or someone else who knew of their technique for giving parties, had thought it necessary that I should attend. And my money was on Olga. Her sudden desire to open her heart to me was a little too sudden, and as for her tears—I shrugged my shoulders at the memory—I had known plenty of tough ladies who had been able to open their tear ducts at will. In fact, I thought Russian women were a damn sight more dangerous when they were crying than otherwise.

Then there was Alexandrov. But I wasn't worrying too much about him. The ex-Hetman of Cossacks hadn't yet realised what he was up against. He was up against Carla. If I knew anything of Carla and her ability to adapt herself to men like Alexandrov he hadn't got a dog's chance.

It took me the best part of three-quarters of an hour to walk home. When I arrived, I made some coffee, drank a small glass of brandy, got into pyjamas and lay down on my bed, smoking and trying to sort out my impressions.

But whatever ideas came into my head I found my mind returning to the delightful and charming Madame St. Philippe, whose entrance into my life and exit from it had been so rapid and without effect. The manner of her death, and her death itself, told me nothing. It was difficult to visualise her as a friend, and a little more difficult to think of her as an enemy.

Unless... and the thought struck me suddenly and I found myself pleased with it... unless Madame St. Philippe was an innocent party in this business who did not know what she was doing. Someone who had been sucked into the little whirlpool caused by the disappearance of Rockie, and who was doing what she was told because she had to. This could easily be. She would not be the first charming and cultured woman who had been blackmailed into working for people she feared and despised.

Whatever I surmised, whatever queer thoughts came into my head, one thing was definite. Both Olly and St. Philippe had been killed to prevent them talking to me. They had to be killed quickly before they had a chance to talk.

                                                    Peter Cheyney

I yawned; got off the bed; went to the window and looked out. It was a still night—or morning. I wondered what Carla was at, and whether she had begun to pump Alexandrov.

I went to sleep.

I was awakened by the telephone jangling in my sitting-room. I got out of bed, reached for a dressing-gown and cursed. I am one of those people who do not like being disturbed—especially by a telephone call—in the small hours of the morning. First of all because I hate the discomfort of waking up, and secondly because nocturnal telephone calls, in my profession, usually mean trouble.

I went into the sitting-room; reached for the telephone.

It was Carla.

She said: "Hallo, Michael... good morning. I'm sorry to disturb you, but you must understand, my dear, that I am in a little trouble; that it was quite necessary for me to disturb you."

I said: "Think nothing of it, my girl." I looked at my watch. It was three-fifteen. I picked up an odd cigarette from the table, and a lighter. I lighted the cigarette and inhaled a mouthful of smoke.

I said: "What is it, Carla? And where are you?"

She answered: "I'm at a place called Forest Hills. At least I'm somewhere on the road between Forest Hills and East Grinstead—but nearer to Forest Hills. There's a cross-roads outside the town and on the right-hand fork there is a telephone box. That's where I am."

"What about Alexandrov?" I asked. "Is he there?"

She said, rather flatly: "He's not here. Not with me. Also, if you please, Michael, I don't want to answer a lot of questions. I am desolate and need sympathy."

I thought that if she was, as she put it, desolate and needing sympathy, something must be very odd and peculiar.

I said: "I'll drive down to you. But it's an hour's journey. What are you going to do in the meantime? You'd better go to an hotel and wait for me."

She said: "No, Michael... that's no good. It is important that no one sees me about here. But I'll go somewhere and I'll come back here and wait for you at the telephone box in an hour's time."

I said: "All right," and hung up.

I dressed quickly, went round to the garage, fuelled the Jaguar and got on to the road. In five minutes' time I was haring down the Fulham Road, indulging in a guesswork competition as to what had happened to Carla.

I kept the speedometer at fifty until I was through Sutton. Then I put my foot down. It was a clear night, the road was clear and I watched the speedometer needle mount up to sixty, seventy, eighty. I relaxed in the driving seat, slowed down to light a cigarette, then accelerated to seventy-five, which is a nice speed for driving and thinking.

I thought that life wasn't so bad if you didn't take it too seriously. That it wasn't too bad even if you did. That you couldn't stop what was going to happen and all you could do was to do your best to see that what happened was as near to what you wanted as you could make it.

                                         Peter Cheyney

This is what I considered to be a good philosophy—provided, I thought with a grin, that Carla hadn't done something to jigger up the whole bag of tricks. Because she was, as you will probably guess, both astute and impulsive, and the two qualities—if you can call them qualities—sometimes do not go very well together.

The moon was shining as I drove through Reigate and swung on to the Eastbourne road. Twenty minutes later I slowed down at the cross-roads outside Forest Hills.

Carla came out of the shadow of an oak tree on the roadside. She held her black velvet cloak and skirts closely about her. I held the car door open for her.

She settled into the passenger seat. She sighed heavily. She said: "Michael, turn the car round and go back towards Forest Hills. Take the last turning to the right down the hill, and keep on driving. Drive until you come to a little white house, set back fifty or sixty yards from the road. Then stop there and put the car somewhere where everyone won't see it."

I said: "All right. What's been going on? And where's Alexandrov?"

She looked at me. I had turned the car and we were back on the main road. Her face was a trifle strained but she was smiling. I thought, quite suddenly and for no reason at all, that she was a damned attractive woman.

She said: "Plenty has been going on, Michael. Alexandrov is dead. I am a little worried and I should like to be kissed."

I put my arm round her and kissed her.

She sighed again. She said: "That was very nice... I

feel better. You know, Michael, I have very great faith in you. Always I consider you to be most reliable."

I said: "Good. Where's Alexandrov... in the little white house?"

She nodded.

"Very well," I said. "We'll go there... fast."

She settled back into her seat. She said: "I suppose he will have to be disposed of somehow. This Alexandrov was a nuisance and a fool... and worse."

I didn't say anything. I lighted a cigarette and asked her if she would like one. She refused. Out of the corner of my eye I could see that she was angry about something.

We ran into Forest Hills and I turned off to the right and continued along the quiet country road. After a few minutes I could see the white house—little more than a cottage—surrounded by a well-kept, fenced-in lawn.

I said: "I'm not going to stop in front. I'll stop here... in this clump of trees. You can approach the house from this side. I'll go down the road, make a circuit and get to the back from the other side. We don't want to be seen together."

"Very well," said Carla. "That method is convenient because the back door is unlocked. I came out that way."

I drove the car off the road into the shadow of the trees; got out and walked down the road keeping in the shadow of the hedge. After I'd passed the house I cut across the fields and made for the back of the white house. Carla was standing by the open back door.

She led the way into the kitchen. I closed the door behind me and followed her through a passageway into

 Peter Cheyney

a room off the hallway in the front of the house.

The room looked out on the side of the house. She switched on the electric light and I saw that the curtains were drawn. The room was comfortably—almost elegantly—furnished. Book-cases filled with well-bound books covered three sides of the wall. Between the windows was an electric fire.

Alexandrov lay between the windows in front of the unlit fire. The cord with the electric fire plug attached was wound round one shoe. A .32 automatic lay a foot or so from him on the carpet.

He was shot through the stomach and he had bled considerably.

Just behind him was a table on which were set out glasses and bottles and an ice bucket filled with water, from which the neck of an unopened bottle of champagne protruded.

I sat down in one of the big saddle-bag chairs. I lighted a cigarette and looked at what remained of Alexandrov. I thought he looked slightly more unpleasant dead than alive.

Carla asked: "D'you want a drink?"

I said: "Why not? I've had a busy evening. And so have you by the look of it. Did you kill him?"

She poured two drinks from a brandy bottle, added some water. She gave me a glass, sat down in the other arm-chair, just behind Alexandrov's head.

"No," she said. "I didn't. But I would have, Michael, with pleasure."

"What happened?" I asked her.

"After you left the party," she said, "he became very

romantic. And he was drinking like a pig. He drank whisky and vodka and God knows what. Also he became bad-tempered and maudlin. In between these things he tried to make love to me—a process which, I am glad to say, consisted mainly of telling me what a hell of a man he was."

"Then he suggested that he take me for a drive. By now the party was over. Everyone was gone and Madame Volanski was drunk and asleep in the little room. I thought it would be good to see where he was going. I thought if he became sufficiently drunk I might get a chance to discover something, because, Michael, all the time I had an odd idea in my head that I have met this Alexandrov somewhere, sometime."

"We got into his car and he drove here, very quickly; the car is parked at the back of the house. We came in here and had drinks. He told me that he owns this house. He told me that he was delighted to have met me because I was just the sort of person he was looking for. First of all because he was fascinated by me, and also because I might be of service to him and make a lot of money for myself in the process."

"He didn't explain how?" I asked.

"He didn't get the chance," she said. "He stopped talking to mix himself another drink. He was standing by the table there and I got a good view of his face from the side. I recognised him in spite of the Cossack moustache. He was no other than Riffenbach, the S.S. Colonel in charge of the concentration camp at Ostrec in Poland. You know I was there. You know how they treated me?"

I nodded.

"He turned and saw the expression on my face," said Carla. "I suppose I looked horrified. And I think that at the same moment he remembered me. He put the glass back on the table; put his hand in the breast pocket of his coat and pulled out the pistol. He turned, took a step towards me and, thank God, tripped over the electric fire cord. He fell heavily and the gun went off. He tried to get up and then fell back and died. I was very pleased when he was dead."

I grinned. "I bet you were." I finished the drink.

"Then I thought I had better get in touch with you," said Carla.

I helped myself to another drink. Then I had a look at Alexandrov.

I opened his coat gingerly and went through his pockets. There was nothing at all but a letter in an opened envelope in one of his side pockets. I put it in my note-case.

I said to Carla. "You get out of here. Take our stiff friend's car and beat it back to town. Go and knock up Glyder. You know where he is?"

She nodded. "Not far from us."

"Give Glyder these instructions from me," I said. "He won't be able to do anything very much until to-night, because it's going to be dawn pretty soon and he can't play about here in the daylight. So we'll have to leave our S.S. friend here for a bit. Tell Glyder that he's to get down here as soon as it's really dark to-night and clean up this mess. He's got to get rid of Riffenbach somehow and in such a manner that he won't be found.

He'll have to destroy the body. And he's got to get rid of that carpet and get another one down and generally clean up the place as if you two had never been here."

"When he's done all that he'd better ring me up and let me know. You'd better leave Riffenbach's car with him too, and tell him to get rid of that when he's finished with it. You understand?"

She nodded. "I will do what you say, Michael. I will leave immediately. You are very kind to me. Always I feel that you are very near to me—like a brother."

She came over and put her arms round my neck. She kissed me— not at all like a brother. Then she went off. A moment or two later I heard the car start up from somewhere at the back of the house.

I went over the house. I pulled all the curtains in all the rooms. Then I began a systematic search. I might have saved myself the trouble. There was nothing that was of any use.

I went back to the sitting-room and took another look at Riffenbach. I thought it rather funny that he should have got through the war, escaped a trial at Nüremberg with a rope at the end of it; got away and talked the Russians into giving him a job, and then, just when everything seemed to be coming his way, he had to shoot himself accidentally in a small white house near Forest Hills.

I helped myself to another drink on him. Then I went home.

# VI. — SONIA

**IT** was a lovely day when I awakened two mornings later. The sun was shining through my bedroom window, making interesting shadows on the carpet. I felt life was pretty good—or was it? On second thoughts I concluded that I wasn't quite certain about that.

I bathed, shaved and dressed, and went out. I began to walk towards Belgrave Square. There was, I thought, an unusual air of cheerfulness about London. Maybe it was the sunshine. All the women I met seemed good-looking, well-dressed and happy. I wondered if they were. I thought it was very interesting to consider what went on in everyone's mind because, whatever you thought about people—especially women—you were usually wrong.

I crossed Belgrave Square; turned off Pont Street into a narrow passageway. Facing me, making the passage a cul-de-sac, was an interesting-looking pub called The Horse With No Legs. I went in; crossed the saloon bar into the bar parlour at the end. It was empty except for the Old Man, who was sitting in the corner wearing a disgruntled expression and a cigar. On the table in front of him was a large glass of port. I ordered a double whisky and soda in the saloon bar, went back to the Old Man and sat down at the other side of the table.

He grunted at me. He said in the peculiarly surly tone of voice which he invariably adopts when someone has asked him to do something: "You're getting to be a bloody nuisance, Kells. Can't you do anything on your own?"

I said: "In this case, no..." I grinned cheerfully at him. "And what are you getting so surly about? You hand me the most impossible jobs with no middle, beginning or ending and expect me to go cavorting through them in forty-eight hours. I'm not Zaza, the mind-reader, you know!"

"I doubt if you have any mind at all," said the Old Man acidly. "Well, what's all the trouble about?"

"There isn't any trouble. All I want is an indication of where we go from here. This thing's beginning to spread a little." I told him what had happened about the cocktail party, about Madame Volanski and the ex-Cossack who wasn't one—Alexandrov.

He said: "So it was Riffenbach? Very interesting. That was the fellow whom the Russians got. So he was working for them?" He looked at me. "What's happened to the body?" he asked.

I drank some of my whisky. "That's taken care of. I sent Glyder down there last night with a drum of vitriol. He used the Haigh process. All that's left of Riffenbach is sludge—out in the back garden well, covered over."

He grunted again. "Well, that's a good thing. Do you know what you are going to do now?"

I nodded. "I found a letter in Riffenbach's pocket. It was from a girl, or woman. Her name is Sabina. Riffenbach was evidently having an affaire with Sabina. If you read the letter you'll see she is a little angry with him." I took the letter from my pocket; handed it to him.

 Peter Cheyney

He read it. "Well?" he queried.

"Just this," I told him. "This Madame Volanski might be anything at all. She was supposed to be Riffenbach's sister. Quite obviously she wasn't. But she's Russian right enough. And if she's Russian she can't very well be Riffenbach's sister. I think she has money. Therefore the question is whether she's some old lady that Riffenbach's picked up somewhere as a cover for himself and a means of financial support, or whether she's something else."

The Old Man said: "Possibly she was put in to keep an eye on Riffenbach. Just so he didn't rat on them. That's not an unusual process of theirs, you know." He took a long pull at his cigar; expelled the smoke slowly and with a great deal of satisfaction. He went on: "You know the Russians never trust anybody. They very often slip up on that fact. They certainly don't trust any of the Nazi German officers who went over to them to escape Nüremberg and a rope. Lots of these Germans have made a getaway. You find 'em all over the world pretending to be Danes and Swedes and all sorts of nationalities. This Madame Volanski might be a Soviet watchdog."

I nodded: "That's what I thought. And she put on a very good act to me of being the rather unfortunate and deluded sister who was worried about her dear brother. She drank a lot of vodka at the party and cried a hell of a lot. She told me that she wanted to ask my advice sometime about her stupid brother who was always getting into trouble. She gave me her telephone number. The idea was that I was to ring her. We were going to lunch together and she was going to talk."

The Old Man said: "Yes, she was probably going to lead you up the garden path, or try to."

"That's what I thought. There is just a possibility, of course, that she wasn't put in by the Russians. Maybe she's just a stupid fool. Maybe he sold her a pup and she was doing her best to play along with him. There's a chance of that."

The Old Man said: "Not much of a chance."

"I agree with you. Anyway, I'm going to see her and I'm going to hear what she's going to say."

He drank some port.

I asked: "Would you think it unreasonable if I asked you to find me a woman—a Russian—from one of your operatives? The idea is this: Riffenbach was having an affaire with this girl. Now we know Volanski wasn't his sister, if our theory is right that the Russians put her in to keep an eye on Riffenbach—and it's my guess that she knew nothing about the affaire he was having with Sabina—what I propose to do is to take a chance on this Sabina—the real Sabina I mean—not turning up. I'm going to put one in, see?"

He nodded. "What you mean is you're going to find some Russian girl and she's going to contact Volanski as the heart-broken young woman who has been seduced by her brother. Is that it?"

"That's it exactly," I said. "But remember, I haven't been in this country very long, and I haven't a long address book of women. You're going to find the Sabina if you don't mind."

"I see..." He finished the port; pushed the glass over to me. "Ask them to fill that again, will you, Kells?"

                                    Peter Cheyney

I took our two glasses into the saloon bar; came back and sat down.

He said: "I've been thinking. There was a young woman did some work for me. She's a White Russian—a Ukrainian. A little bit excitable, but very loyal. Her name's Sonia Karakoff."

"That's all right. Where do I find Sonia, and will she play ball?"

He said: "Yes... She worked for us during the war. She's quite a dependable person. She's part proprietor of a night club on the other side of Maidenhead. It's called the Yellow Penguin. I think it's a little bit near the knuckle, but they seem to keep on the right side of the police."

I said: "I'll go and see her. Supposing she won't play?"

He took a long drag on his cigar. "I thought of that. You'd better take the car. Go down to my place and see Miss Fains. She has a dossier on Sonia. This Sonia is very much in love with a man called Mellish—a funny type but apparently attractive to women. Anyway, he's attracted Sonia. You'd better pull the black on her somehow; then she'll have to work for you. That should be easy enough, shouldn't it? But leave me out of it if you can. I may need her again sometime and she can be very bad-tempered if she wants to."

I said: "And I'll try and find Mellish. Maybe Miss Fains will know where he is. I'll sell him a story that I'm a Home Office official; that somebody has discovered something not so good about Sonia, and she's up for deportation. I take it she wouldn't like to go back to Russia, would she?"

The Old Man shook his head. "She'd do anything not to go back there."

"All right. It's a pretty lousy way to work, isn't it?"

The Old Man yawned. "It's a pretty lousy world. Incidentally, have you begun to get squeamish in your old age?"

I grinned at him. "The end is always worthy of the means. I'd better get down to your place."

He said: "Do... and get it over. I don't want you hanging around there. Some of your past exploits have given you a little too much publicity."

"I won't be there long," I assured him. "I'll drive down there now, see Fains, ask her for Mellish's address and get to work."

He asked: "What's the idea of putting the supposed Sonia in on Volanski?"

"This: I see Volanski and find out what it is she wants my advice about. I'm not going to tell her Riffenbach has disappeared. I'll tell her a story about his having taken a powder and got out of it; that he's got in trouble over some woman, and see what her reaction is to this. And if it sounds all right; then Sabina alias Sonia Karakoff appears, weeps on Volanski's shoulder; tells her she has been seduced by her brother Alexandrov, alias Riffenbach. And then we'll see what happens. Maybe Volanski is going to do a little talking. Maybe she'll try to use Sonia. We'll just sit around and watch."

The Old Man shrugged his shoulders. "You've got some goddam funny ways of working."

"Maybe. But most of my goddam funny ways have come off, as you know. If you don't like it what else

                                    Peter Cheyney

do I do?"

He grunted. "How do I know? All right. You'd better go down and see Fains."

"Thanks," I said. I got up. "I'll be seeing you."

He looked up at me. "But as little as possible, if you don't mind, Kells. And another thing, don't try to lay Fains. She's never been the same woman since the night she kept that date with you."

I said: "You've got the wrong idea. I made the date, but I didn't keep it. I was busy working for you, so I had to cancel it. She's never had any sort of explanation, so I suppose she's got the needle."

"Whatever your alibi may be—and I've never known you not to have an excuse—lay off Fains. She's too valuable to me to have her mentality upset by your amorous approaches. One day some woman is going to be the death of you."

I said: "What a death! So long, sir..."

I went away.

**I ARRIVED** at the Old Man's place just after two. I rang the bell and told the maid I wanted to see Miss Fains. She led the way to the back of the house where Fains' den was. The maid opened the door and disappeared. I went inside.

Fains' room was a sight. A mixture of feminine taste and almost appalling efficiency. It was a long, "L" shaped room, and one end of the "L" was filled from floor to ceiling with green filing cases. These were the Old Man's for private records. There were flowers, freshly gathered, all over the place, and copies of Vogue and a few extra-romantic novels.

The room looked like Fains—an attractive mixture of romance, efficiency and femininity.

She was sitting at a long refectory table covered with papers, typing a report.

I said: "Hallo, Fainits...."

She said: "I wish you wouldn't call me 'Fainits.' I'm Miss Fains to you."

I said: "I know, Fainits. And you have a lovely name. I've always adored Aurora and I think the name Aurora Fains is something, and so are you!"

And she was. She had a round face and rather a lovely shade of blonde hair—the same colour as a cornfield. She wore pince-nez, which made her blue eyes look a trifle severe but gave a peculiarly attractive angle to a face that would normally have been very simple. Also she had a nice mouth and teeth. Beyond that, she ran pretty true to form except that her legs were definitely handsome. She knew this and always wore the right kind of sheer nylon stockings and attractive American shoes with very high heels.

She said: "Mr. Kells, what is it you want. Does the Old Man know you're down here?"

"Of course. I saw him this morning. I told him that life was just one big desert without you. If you'd heard what I said about you, you'd have blushed to the roots of that lovely hair."

She said: "Kells, you're just about the biggest damn' liar I've ever met and I've met a few."

I raised my eyebrows. "Why?"

She said: "You know I never go out with men...

                                        Peter Cheyney

anyway, not often. You work on me for weeks. Do you remember when the Old Man sent me over to France to do some work for you? And you make a big date and you never turned up. I'm not used to being stood up by people like you. I don't think I like you very much."

I spread my hands. "I know... Do you know why I couldn't turn up to meet you? I was on my way to keep the appointment when I was set on by five men."

She said: "Good heavens... What did they do?"

"Didn't you know?" I asked. "I don't believe you take the slightest interest in me, my sweet. You just don't care what happens to me and whether I'm dead or alive."

She asked in a rather more concerned voice: "Well, what did happen?"

"They killed me and I was found dead the next morning with my throat cut. And you wonder why I didn't keep my appointment."

She said: "You're impossible. What is it you really want?"

"I'll tell you." I walked round the table and kissed her. She struggled but not too much. She stood looking at me reproachfully.

I said: "Well, Fainits, having got the main business of the afternoon over, get cracking on some of those funny green boxes of yours. I want to know all you've got on a Russian lady named Sonia Karakoff, and if your file is properly cross-indexed this will lead you on to some man called Mellish, who is enamoured of Sonia. Let me have a note on both dossiers, so that I can go away and study it, and I'll be very much obliged to you. And get a move on because, as you know, the Old Man doesn't like me being seen around here."

She said: "Neither do I."

"You may not, my sweet," I told her. "But one day you'll feel different. On some misty morning when you all stand round my graveside and the bugles play the Last Post and there is an air of indefinable sadness over everything, you will think of me and weep."

She said: "Like hell I will...!"

She went over to the files. I sat down on a chair and smoked a cigarette.

**IT** was just after six. I was sitting in a big chair with a cigarette and a long drink, looking out at the Knightsbridge traffic, when Glyder arrived. He helped himself to a whisky and soda, put a piece of ice in the glass, looked at it intently and, finding it to his satisfaction, drank some.

He said: "Good evening, Mike."

I said: "Good evening. Have a drink?"

"Thanks, I will..." He finished the glass and poured himself another one.

I said: "That's a very good system of drinking."

"It's not too bad," he said. "It always puts me one drink ahead of anyone else." He helped himself to a cigarette; pulled up a chair; sat down.

"Well, what about it?" I asked.

He said: "I went to the Foreign Office this afternoon. I saw Woldingham. He was very helpful. This Sonia Karakoff is quite a piece."

I asked: "How?"

He said: "Sonia Karakoff is thirty-two. She was born in the early part of the Russian Revolution. Her father was a Czarist general. Her mother came of a very good family. The Bolsheviks didn't like them, and sent the General and his wife to Siberia. Sonia was born there. She doesn't like Bolsheviks. She's done all sorts of good work over here. She once did a job for M.I.5 and I understand she's been a help on one or two occasions to the Special Branch. She did quite a bit of work for the Old Man in the latter part of the war. She's temperamental, but she can be trusted."

"I see..." I looked at him. Glyder was a strange sort of egg. He was a Devonshire man. He had a small farm somewhere near Bolt Head in South Devon. He was in the Devonshire regiment in the 1914-18 war. When he volunteered for the last war there was something physically wrong with him, so they wouldn't have him. In the middle of the war he went for a holiday somewhere on the coast. He spent his time wandering about the beaches at night, in spite of the fact that they were wired off and there were sentries all over the place. I rather think that Glyder, who was inclined to be slightly romantic and mysterious, liked dodging these sentries and tried to see just how far he could go into places where he ought not to go. So one night he won something. Two or three German naval details landed in a small boat from a submarine. They knocked Glyder over the head and took him back with them—what for I don't know.

Apparently the Germans, who can be pretty stupid on occasion, got the idea in their heads that Glyder was quite a big shot, mainly, I suppose, because they'd found him in a forbidden area on the east coast. They didn't do anything to him except that he was kicked about from prison to prison, and eventually he managed to escape. But whilst he'd been in Germany he'd kept his eyes open. He'd learned an awful lot. He'd also learnt German and when he got back to England via Switzerland he had secured a mine of valuable information, so much so that he was eventually sent to see the Old Man.

Glyder had never left the Old Man. He'd gone on working for him from that time—pretty good work, too. He had the nerve of the devil, and a peculiar mental quirk that was more than astuteness. He still had his farm near Bolt Head, but someone else was running it. He used to go back there for a fortnight each year on holiday. During the rest of the year he took the devil's own chances. Candidly, my opinion of him was that he was much more clever than he allowed us to believe.

He was about five-feet ten, thin but wiry. And as strong as a horse. The one rather extraordinary thing about him was that he never looked at a woman, although women fell for him. I rather fancy that Glyder thought that if he fell for some attractive member of the other sex he might talk too much when he'd had a drink. He liked drinking.

I asked: "Did you get anything on Mellish?"

He said: "There's nothing on the files in the Foreign Office. He might have a police record."

I said: "Tell me about the Karakoff. What's her nationality?"

"She's still a White Russian," said Glyder. "There's an

                                    Peter Cheyney

application in—and I understand it's going through—for her British naturalisation. The Old Man recommended it."

I grinned. "That's damned funny."

Glyder looked at me sideways. "What are you doing—putting the black on her to work for you? You're a ruthless bastard, aren't you, Mike?"

I said: "You tell me what else I do. Somebody's got to do the work, haven't they?"

"I suppose so." He helped himself to another drink. He asked: "Would you like a drink?"

I said: "Thanks. I'd better have one before the bottle's empty. Tell me about Riffenbach."

He said: "Believe it or not that Riffenbach was a brute to dispose of. That fellow took two drums of vitriol and before I was through with it I was very glad I had a gas mask on. I worked right past the dawn with my knees knocking together all the time in case the milkman came in and saw Riffenbach's legs sticking over the top of the iron tub. That would have been a nice situation, wouldn't it—nice for the milkman?"

I said: "But it's all right."

"Yes, nobody's going to find anything of him. The last bit had gone when I phoned you—even his teeth."

I asked: "Was he wearing any dentures?"

He said: "He hadn't got dentures. Really, he wasn't a bad- looking man." He held out my drink.

I took the glass from him. I asked: "Where's this Mellish?"

"Search me," said Glyder. "I know where his office is, but he's not there. Apparently he's in the fruit business—at least he has an office near Covent Garden as an agent for dried fruits or something. There was nobody working in the office. I think he goes there for about an hour a day. I saw the caretaker. She didn't know a thing. She said he was usually gone by the afternoon; that he was a nice man considering he was a foreigner, and very generous."

I said: "That's interesting. I bet his name isn't Mellish. He's probably using the name. That's tough. He might have a record."

He said: "Well, give me a day or so and I'll find him. Is there anything else you want?"

I said: "Not particularly. Are you doing anything?"

He grinned. "I'm supposed to be working on a beautiful woman spy. She's one of those silly dames that the Reds put the screw on. You know, they get sent out in dozens to every country in the world. They're usually good-looking but stupid. The idea is, as you know, that they might discover something and if they don't, after a certain time, they cut their money off. What happens to them after that I don't know."

I said: "Well, stick around. I'll phone through when I want you. And don't be too hard on the beautiful spy."

He said: "So long, Mike..." and went away.

I went out and had some dinner at the Hyde Park Hotel. Then I walked round and got the Jaguar out of the garage. I drove down to Maidenhead. On the way down I amused myself by thinking about Miss Sonia Karakoff. I thought it was very true that half the world doesn't know how the other half lives, and I wondered just how many women of all sorts, shapes and descriptions—White Russians, displaced persons, women who'd been leading normal decent lives in Roumania, Poland, Hungary—all with the usual ideals of home, husband and children—were being kicked around the world, spying, looking through key-holes and generally raising hell at the behest of the beneficent Soviet. I thought it was rather extraordinary, having regard to all things, that they were so trustworthy. For quite a lot of them were. This brought me to the thought that when you get down to bed-rock women have a surplus of ideals. Maybe it is because they are more romantic. Maybe it is because they are a little more determined... I don't know. But they certainly put up with a lot.

I found the Yellow Penguin. It was just outside Maidenhead, at the end of a long country road which contained only a few large houses, not big enough to be a nuisance to their owners and not small enough to be unnoticeable. At the end of this road on the right hand side were two imposing iron gates. There was a carriage drive which led to the front of the club. I left the car half-way down the drive in the shadow of some trees; finished the journey on foot.

The club was attractive; the grounds well-kept. The double front doors were open and I walked into an attractive, square hall furnished with good solid mahogany and a few fake antiques.

A weedy-looking individual, dressed as a butler, came out of a side door. He said: "Good evening, sir. Can I do anything for you? I don't think you're a member, are you?"

I said: "No, I'm not a member, and I'm not a policeman, so don't be uneasy. I'd like very much to have
a few words with Miss Sonia Karakoff. The name's
Michael Kells."

"Very well, sir. I'll go and find the Countess."

I lighted a cigarette and waited.

After a few minutes my weedy friend returned. He
said: "Will you come this way, sir?"

I threw my cigarette stub into a brass ash-tray and
went after him. We seemed to walk a long way down
one passage and up another. From here and there about
the house I could hear the sound of music and voices.
Eventually, he pulled aside a heavy plush curtain and
opened a door. I went into the room.

She was standing in front of the fireplace. A small
fire was burning, either for effect or because there was a
little breeze in the air. The room was well-furnished in
dark oak. The pile carpet was a soft blue. Two or three
vases were filled with well-arranged flowers. It was a nice
room.

She said: "Good evening to you. I am the Countess
Sonia Karakoff." She smiled.

I am going to tell you that the Countess—as she
called herself—Sonia Karakoff was definitely easy on the
eyes. She was tall—about five feet nine—and she had
one of those faces that one is never quite certain about.
She had a camelia complexion and a raspberry mouth.
The shape of her face was fascinating. You looked at
her and wondered whether she was lovely or pretty or
merely handsome. She had a straight, long nose: full,
attractive lips; large dark eyes. Her hair was dead black

and dressed closely to her head. She wore a close-fitting, long, lace dinner frock and high heeled crêpe-de-Chine sandals. Round her neck was a necklace of cabochon emeralds, and there was a bracelet to match for each slim wrist. Her fingers were long and white. She must have worn at least ten rings on her hands, and one of them in diamonds was a replica of the Cross of St. George of Russia. She was definitely an eyeful.

I said: "Good evening to you, Countess. My name's Michael Kells, and I thought it was time you and I had a little talk."

She said, without moving: "About what, Mr. Kells?"

I came a little closer. "You know, I think it's time that you went back to work. So does the Old Man."

She smiled. Her teeth were white and even. She smiled only with her mouth. Her eyes were steady and watchful.

She said: "So...! But I thought it was understood that that part of my life was finished. You see, I now own this club. I am very interested in it. It is successful. Here I exist in the peace of the countryside. Sometimes I look at the birds, and there are other things..."

I said: "I'd still like to talk to you."

She sighed. "I am a weak woman. And you look to me like a very determined man. Also I have heard about you, Mr. Kells." She smiled again. She went on: "Would you like to drink with me? Tell me what you would like. Will you drink champagne or brandy or whisky or rum or vodka?"

I asked: "Are you going to drink vodka?"

"No, I shall drink brandy."

I said: "Well, I'll drink brandy, too."

"Please help yourself to cigarettes, which you will find on the table." She rang a bell by the fireplace. When the weedy- looking butler arrived she ordered brandy, soda and ice.

I walked about the room, smoking a cigarette and looking at the pictures. They were pretty good and there were some excellent, carefully chosen prints. We didn't say anything. She stood relaxed, almost inanimate, in front of the fire, her hands clasped loosely behind her back, her head up, her eyes following me as I walked round the room. I took a quick look at her over my shoulder. In that position a very good figure showed itself to the best advantage, and the plunging neckline of her frock told the world that the "Countess" Sonia Karakoff had no need of uplift.

The butler put the drinks on the table and went away.

She said: "Let us sit down and talk."

I placed a chair for her, poured out the drinks; added soda and ice and put them on the table. We sat down.

I said: "I expect you know what I am here for. In our peculiar profession, Countess—and I have an idea that you know more about me than you care to tell—wars go on for ever, even when the shooting stops."

She said languidly: "Has that stopped? It seems to me that somewhere in the world there is always shooting." She drank a little brandy fastidiously. Then she said: "I wish I had a machine-gun so that I could go out into the world and shoot everybody except myself and those I love."

I said: "I can't see what good that would do."

                                        Peter Cheyney

"Perhaps not...! What is it that you wish me to do? And why should I do it?"

I said: "Sonia, I'm going to be very frank with you. You have an application in at the Home Office for British nationality, and on your record you certainly deserve it. Incidentally, that application was recommended by the Old Man. It would be rather a pity if he should be forced to withdraw his recommendation. If he did I don't think there would be any naturalisation for you."

She said: "I see... blackmail...! Do you know, Kells, what I think you are—a complete and utter swine?"

"Maybe... Why don't you call me Michael? But that is the position. I think that the Old Man rather feels that you ought to do one more job. After that, I give you my word that that application is going through right away. Before you know where you are you'll find yourself a British citizen."

She asked: "What is this business? Do I have to go away. Do I have to be at the mercy of some Bolshevik or some German Nazi?"

I said: "That's the charm of the whole thing, Sonia. I don't think you'll have to go anywhere. I don't think you'll have to go outside London, and probably you'll be able to run your club at the same time."

Her eyes widened. "This is amazing. This is what you call too good to be true." Her voice was soft, a little hoarse, very attractive. "This sounds almost likeable. Before, I have been asked to do much more difficult things."

I said: "This may be difficult, even if you don't have to travel, and there's just as much danger in England as there is in some other parts of the world. You know what our friends on the other side are like."

She said softly: "I know." She went on: "Very much I wish to have my British nationality; also I would always like to oblige the Old One. Incidentally, I would like also to be friends with you. But there is the question of love to be considered. I am in love."

I said: "That's too bad."

She went on: "You see I am always in love. One must always be in love to get any sort of inspiration from life. Whatever one does is always done better if one is in love—even working for the Old One. Love is inclined to improve one's technique."

I asked: "Exactly what is this leading to?"

She said: "I have a person in this club. His name is Rico Mellish—or that is what he calls himself. He is very excitable. He is not likely to approve of any scheme that you wish to put up to me."

"No one's asking him to approve of anything. My advice to him is to watch his step if he's going to butt into my business. Where is this Mellish?"

She said: "He is here. Perhaps you would like to meet him before you go." She stopped talking as the door was burst open.

A man came into the room. I guessed this was Mellish. He was tall and thin. He had a thin face—a face with a grudge against the world. He was inclined to be sallow. Under his nose was a pencil-line moustache, a not particularly nice mouth and large white teeth. He had lots of black hair that was plastered down in the fashion that gigolos adopt. His double-breasted tuxedo fitted him too well and his shirt and collar were of the finest silk. His patent leather evening shoes were too pointed. There were rings on his fingers. He looked to me rather a dangerous type.

He slammed the door. Without looking at me he came across to the table and addressed Sonia. He talked to her in Russian, spitting the words out of his mouth.

She said languidly: "My Rico, you might just as well talk English. I am sure that Mr. Kells speaks Russian."

He gesticulated violently with his hands. He said in an Italian accent: "Very well, I will speak English. They tell me that this man come to the house to-night and demanded to see you. This is behind my back. So you don't trust me. You have no faith in me." He pointed a long, well-manicured forefinger at me. "So this man is your lover?"

Sonia rose slowly to her feet. She said: "My darling, you are becoming excited. Come here, my sweet one." She picked up the brandy bottle and hit him across the face.

Mellish subsided on the carpet unconscious.

She put the bottle back on the tray. She said, apologetically: "You understand, Michael, that Rico is a little passionate and violent. On these occasions the only thing to do is to arrange for him to go to sleep. When he comes to I will reason with him. In the meantime let us walk in the garden. It is pleasant there."

I got up. I felt that I was going to like the Countess Karakoff.

We went into the garden.

# V. — VOLANSKI

**AT** eleven o'clock I looked up the telephone number Madame Volanski had given me and called her. A few moments later Volanski came on the line.

I reminded her that she had asked me to get into touch with her; would she like to lunch with me?

She said no; she'd like me to lunch with her. She suggested that we met at a restaurant in Soho. She said the food was very good there; that she was glad I'd called her. She sounded rather down, I thought... I imagined she was either in the throes of a deep depression or suffering from a first-class hangover.

I found her a rather difficult person to think about, more especially because you never know about women. And, believe me, you don't! They are the greatest dissemblers in creation and the soft, shy little woman who can't say boo to a goose can be as dangerous and pack as mean a wallop as the most veritable Amazon. Right from the start I'd found Madame Volanski rather more than an enigma. Outwardly, she was a fat, peculiarly shapeless, miserable Russian type. She was in fact an old bag, but then you never knew even when they were old bags, when they were Russians. The question that was uppermost in my mind was whether Volanski knew that her pretended brother, Alexandrov, the ex-Hetman of Cossacks, was Riffenbach, late of the S.S., now working for the Russians. Of course she might know that. She might have picked Riffenbach up somewhere and joined forces with him in order to keep an eye on him, or she might not. Riffenbach, with his big, burly frame, immense moustaches and complete self-confidence, would not be unattractive to a certain type of woman. And apparently Volanski had money. It might be that. I shrugged my shoulders. It wasn't any good asking myself questions. I had to try and find out.

I went out at one o'clock and found the restaurant. It was a small place—not far from the Tottenham Court Road. It was long, narrow, airless, and smelt vaguely of garlic. The tablecloths weren't very clean and the waiters might have been anything but waiters.

I went in. She was sitting at a table in the corner at the end of the room. She looked terrible. She was wearing a tight, black coat and skirt which would have looked fashionable on anyone else's figure, but not on hers. Her ample bosom was endeavouring to escape from the tightness of the coat. Her fat, shapeless face was covered with about an eighth of an inch of enamel, and her eyes—small and beady through crying or a hangover, I didn't know which—looked miserably around the over-heated room. She wore a funny hat under which some wisps of hair had escaped, and on one lapel of her coat was a large diamond clip that must have been worth five thousand pounds.

I said: "Good morning, Madame Volanski. How is it? You don't look very well. Are you still worrying about your brother?"

She said, in a low, cracked voice: "Call me Olga. Of course I'm terribly worried. Always I worry. All the time I look around for 'appiness and what do I always get?

What you call a poke in the eye."

I said: "You'd better have a hair of the dog that bit you. You were crying last night, weren't you? What was it—vodka?"

She said: "My friend, you are right. You are a man of discernment. I wish I knew some more about you. You are mysterious, but I theenk you have a peculiar sort of wisdom. It was not only vodka. It was misery and tears. Always they go together."

I signalled to one of the waiters—a rather decrepit specimen- -who shuffled over; ordered two large brandies and sodas and handed the menu to her.

She said: "I do not want to eat. I am miserable."

"A little food won't hurt." I ordered for us both.

She said: "I don' know why I wanted to talk to you, but a woman gets to a state when she feels she 'as to do something. She is 'arassed and miserable. She is excited and lonely and impatient."

"I know..." I grinned at her. "Ladies won't wait," I said, rather liking the implication of those words. "They think there's nothing worth waiting for, so they feel they have to do something about it."

She said: "Yes. They 'ave to do something about it. But what are they to do? What does a woman do when she is lonely and sick for love and she does not trust anybody? What is she to do, Mister Kells?"

I gave her a cigarette; lighted it; took one myself.

I said: "You can take it from me that the best thing she can do is to trust somebody even if she is wrong."

"I would like to trust you," she said. "But I am rather afraid of you."

                                    Peter Cheyney

"Yes? What are you afraid of me for?"

She shrugged her shoulders. "There could be a lot of reasons. You might be a policeman. You might be a spy. You might be anything."

I said: "All right. Let's examine that. If I'm a policeman why should you be afraid of the fact, and why should you expect me to be a spy?"

She shrugged her shoulders again. "I am not thinking for myself. I am thinking for Alexandrov." Tears welled into her eyes. It struck me that her affection for the supposed Alexandrov was almost too strong for a sister.

I asked: "I suppose he is your brother?"

She shook her head. "No... 'e is not my brother. If 'e was my brother I would not cry. I don' know why I am telling you of this, but I 'ave 'ad enough of everything. I 'ave to talk to somebody. 'E is not my brother. 'E is my lover. I adored 'eem. Not only is 'e my lover; 'e is also a sadist. You see, this son of a beech knew my temperament. You know, Russian women are always the same, wherever they come from. They like being 'urt and Alexandrov is an expert at doing that. 'E telephones to girls in front of me and makes appointments. Once I threw a bronze statue at 'eem. I missed 'eem and 'e threw it back at me and knocked two front teeth out. I was in agony for weeks. 'E laughed at me when I came back from the dentist's and said it was necessary to suffer in order to be beautiful, and that the new teeth looked better than the old ones.

"Always 'e is going off to some place 'e 'as somewhere—a place about which I knew nothing—and taking women. This pleases 'eem. 'E knows it drives me mad. Eventually, I came to realise that all 'e wants from me is my money."

"What is he doing here?" I asked. "According to what you told me the other night you two have been wandering about the world, and being kicked out of country after country. Was that true? According to you, you exist merely to supply money to this man much younger than yourself whom you love."

She looked at me. Tears were trembling in her eyes. Her mascara'd eyelids were fluttering. Across the table came a suggestion of stale breath.

I thought Volanski was a terrible woman. I thought that Riffenbach was more than a trifle heroic to stand for her. He must have wanted the money badly.

She said: "I theenk you are a police officer or something like that. Why should I talk any more to you?"

I replied: "I don't know. I'll make one or two guesses. Have you got your passport with you, Olga?"

She looked at me quickly. I saw a suggestion of fear in her eyes. She answered: "I 'ave not my passport with me. Alexandrov 'as my passport."

I thought that was pretty good. I said: "Well, it looks as if you're in a spot, Olga, because Alexandrov has gone and your passport with him. I wouldn't like to be you."

She said: "My God... 'ere is some more misery...! Always I am followed by a relentless fate." She cried some more; then took a large gulp of brandy and soda. There was a silence. I looked at her. I thought that even if Olga Volanski liked being miserable the news about Riffenbach had definitely shaken her badly.

                    Peter Cheyney

She said: "Tell me about 'eem. Where 'as 'e gone?"

I decided to take a chance. I said: "I'm going to trust you, Olga, because you told me the truth about Alexandrov not being your brother. Well, I'm an Aliens Officer at the Passport Office. When I received your invitation to the cocktail party I didn't know that I was going to meet Alexandrov there. I was very lucky, because we've been very interested in him and his movements. Are you sure you don't know what he was doing? What he really came to England for?"

"No..." She took out a lace handkerchief delicately perfumed; dabbed at her eyes, being careful not to disturb the mascara. "I met Alexandrov in Egypt. We met at a gaming 'ouse. I love gambling. I am a rich woman, but I am always losing my money. I took a liking to 'eem, and 'e professed to be ver' fond of me. I expect it was my money. So we joined forces and became brother and sister. Then we went to Paris. Something 'appened and 'e said we must get out; we must go to England."

I asked: "How did you get into England?"

"I do not know. We came over on the boat, and 'e produced the necessary papers and passports. Where 'e got them from I do not know. I was so crazy about 'eem that I did not ask any questions. Then there was a woman who owned a dress shop. Alexandrov seemed to know 'er. He told me to say that was my business; that I was in the dressmaking business, if anybody asked me. The invitations to that party were arranged for by the dress shop. I do not know who did it. Alexandrov 'ad the apartment in St. John's Wood. Where 'e got it from I do not know. 'E told me 'e also 'ad a 'ouse somewhere in the country."

I looked at her again. I wondered if she was telling the truth. Actually, I believed she was.

She went on: "Now you see 'ow impossible is my situation. I 'ave no passport. I 'ave no friends. I am living in this apartment at St. John's Wood, about which I know nothing, and now you tell me that 'e 'as gone... that damned 'andsome beast...!"

I said: "Well, if it's any consolation to you, Olga, you won't be the only woman who is upset. There was somebody else."

"Yes...?" she queried. "Tell me... who else? Is she beautiful? I would like to keel 'er. I would like to get my fingers round 'er throat and tear 'er eyes out."

I said: "Very understandable. I'm afraid she is rather good- looking, and I think that Alexandrov was a little afraid of her. You see, he'd seduced her and then I think tried to give her the air. I've an idea that she threatened him, and he decided that the easiest thing to do would be to get out."

She said in a low voice: "Who is this woman?"

"I don't know. That's what I want to find out. All I know about her is that her name is Sabina. Does that mean anything to you?"

She shook her head. "It means nothing." She shrugged her shoulders again. "Probably there were other women."

I said: "I expect there were, but I think this one was rather important."

She said: "I want some brandy. And tell them to take this food away. It makes me ill."

                    Peter Cheyney

I called the waiter; ordered more brandy and soda. I told him to take my plate away, but I didn't tell him that it also made me feel ill. She relapsed into silence; sank back in her chair, looking like a bundle.

She said: "I would like to know about you. You told me that you are of the Aliens Office. You come to me and you tell me these things. Why?"

The waiter brought the brandies and sodas. I picked up my glass and drank; gave myself time for a little thinking.

I said: "My business is to check up on aliens who get into this country who don't register with the police; who have illegal passports, or no passports at all."

"And you could make things very unpleasant for me?" she asked. "I suppose you could send me to prison. You could do anything you like?"

"Practically... But I don't want to do that. I want to do something else."

She raised her eyebrows. "Yes...? What is it you want to do?"

I did some quick thinking. I've already said you never know where you are with women. I've already said I'd an idea she was telling the truth, but I didn't know that. I decided to take a chance, because if you're handling a situation which you know very little about, as I knew very little about the situation confronting me, the best thing you can do is to risk it.

I said: "I'll tell you what the situation is exactly, Olga. Let's talk about your supposed brother, who was your lover—the ex-Hetman of Cossacks, Alexandrov. Would you be surprised if I were to tell you that his name was

Riffenbach; that he was an ex-Colonel of the S.S.; that at one time he was in charge of a concentration camp in Poland?"

She said: "My God! But 'e speaks Russian perfectly. 'E 'as the background."

"I know all that," I replied. "He probably spoke Russian and has been there for some time—since before the ending of the war when he was captured by the Russians. This man was working for the Soviets."

She hissed through her teeth: "So...! Those Bolshevists... If I 'ad known this... if I were to tell you what these people did to my family. 'Ow I 'ate them..." She was practically foaming at the mouth with rage.

I said: "That's not so good, is it? Now let me tell you what I think about this girl Sabina."

She leaned forward. Her eyes brightened. She was interested. I think she was definitely telling the truth when she said she'd like to get her hands on Sabina.

I went on: "I'm telling you about this Sabina whom I know you don't like very much, because you might like to help me. This is what I believe. When Riffenbach came here with you Sabina was already here. He'd known her before—probably in Russia. I believe that she's working for the Russian Government; that she was over here to keep an eye on Riffenbach; to see that he carried out whatever assignment it was he'd been given. You know that's their system, especially with a man like Riffenbach who wasn't Russian and who once he was out of that country might try some funny business. You know they always have someone else to keep an eye on people like that. It's my considered opinion that the

                                    Peter Cheyney

person was Sabina. Maybe she had pretended to fall for Riffenbach. But there's no doubt about it that your late lover has taken his chance and got out."

She asked: "Do you think 'e 'as got out of this country?"

I nodded. "He's certainly not here."

She said: "Of course, you know, 'e is clever. Underneath all those moustaches and that air 'e puts on to impress women there is a good brain. 'E as taken 'is chance and got out. 'E 'as left me 'ere like a rat."

I asked: "Where did you get your money from, Olga?"

"I got it from America. I am an American citizen. I 'ad an American passport, but I 'ave not got it now. Of course 'e 'as stolen it. Sometime or other it is going to be useful to 'eem."

I said: "I see... Well, it's all very simple, isn't it. What are you going to do, Olga?"

"It is what you want me to do, is it not?" she asked. "What chance 'ave I 'ere—a lonely woman. What is it you want?"

I said: "Isn't it conceivable that as you came over here with Riffenbach you were also working for the Soviets. Anyway, that's going to be your story, because if you can get this woman Sabina to believe that is the truth she is going to talk to you, isn't she? She's not going to talk to you if she knows you're a White Russian with an American passport; that you loathe the Bolshevists. Another thing is this, it is on the cards that Riffenbach never mentioned your name to her. Probably he was supposed to come over here by himself. It is more probable that he picked you up merely because you were a rich woman and he needed money to make his getaway. Has he any money of yours?"

She said: "'E 'as plenty. Not only 'as 'e money; 'e 'as jewellery which I gave 'eem—evening sets and cuff links, a platinum watch and a lovely cigarette case. 'E 'as 'ad thousands of dollars from me."

I nodded. "You can take it that that's the truth, Olga. He's got your money. He's made his getaway and Sabina is in a very nasty frame of mind. If my guess is right and she's working for the Bolshevists, she's going to find herself in a spot when she reports that the man she was supposed to keep an eye on and look after has got away."

She said: "Tell me what to do."

I lighted a cigarette; leaned over the table. I said: "Listen, Sabina is going to try and find out about things, isn't she? She must have known where Riffenbach was living. She's going to make inquiries. It's ten to one she has other associates here. Eventually, in order to try and find out where he's gone, she's coming to see you, isn't she?"

She nodded her head.

I went on: "Your story to her is that Riffenbach suddenly disappeared. You don't know where he has gone to. But you're very angry about the whole thing."

She said: "Yes... yes... I follow you..."

I continued: "She's going to try and pump you. She's going to try and find out everything you know about Riffenbach, but in doing so she'll probably have to give something away herself. Listen carefully to everything

                    Peter Cheyney

she tells you. I'll make an appointment to see you again. You can give me your news. Directly she gets in touch with you—because I am certain she will get in touch with you—make an appointment to see her, and ring me up. You understand?"

She said slowly: "Yes, I understand. If I succeed, what will you do for me?"

"I'll do two things, Olga. I'll get you a passport and I'll arrange that you can stay here or, if you like, go back to France. And I'll do something that you'll like even more. I'll have Sabina arrested."

She smiled at me. "That ees the greatest inducement. I'd like that. Very well, M'sieu Kells. I will wait till she comes to me. I will be clever with 'er like a snake. You understand? Then I will ring you. Nothing would please me more than that this woman Sabina should be arrested. I would like 'er to rot in prison."

I said: "Finish your drink, and I'll drop you at home. Where do you want to go?"

"I want to go to the apartment at St. John's Wood. When I get there I am going to dreenk a whole bottle of vodka. I am going to forget my worries."

I said: "You wouldn't be cock-eyed when Sabina appears—if she does appear?"

"No... I will be cool and calm and calculating. I will be like a snake...."

I paid the bill and drove Olga to her apartment in St. John's Wood. Then I went home.

**I WAS** drinking tea when Glyder rang the door-bell of my apartment. I let him in; pointed to the sideboard. He helped himself.

He said: "I've been down to see the Old Man. He seems very interested in you and what you're doing.

"That's very nice of him," I said. "He didn't send you up here to tell me that, did he?"

He shook his head. "I was to tell you that he remembered you talked to him about a woman called Theodora St. Philippe. You'd met her in Paris. He said that he had a roving agent working in the Russian Sector in Germany. Her name was Hermione Martin and he said he has the idea that she'd managed to get in rather closely with the other side."

I said: "Oh, yes—a double agent. A nasty job for a woman."

"He says she's a very beautiful woman," said Glyder, "who was used to taking a lot of chances, because she was very fond of her husband. The Jerries got him and he died in a concentration camp. I suppose she was trying to get her own back."

I nodded.

"The Old Man says he's heard nothing of her," Glyder went on, "and he's had a tip from Germany. She's disappeared or is dead or something like that. He thought maybe you'd like to tie this thing up with Theodora St. Philippe."

I said: "All right. I've got that." My mind went back to Theodora St. Philippe lying on the bed in her apartment with her head smashed in. I thought it was all the tea in China to a bad egg that this was Hermione Martin—the Old Man's double agent who had disappeared. I thought that would explain a lot.

    

I asked: "Was that all he had to tell me? And what was all the hurry about?"

Glyder said: "I think that the hurry is tied up somehow with the arrival yesterday at Dover of a man called Everard Mailey Jane. The Old Man said that after his conversation with you he'd had the ports watched. This Jane came over yesterday from Calais on the Invicta. He stayed last night at the White Cliffs Hotel. This morning he came up to London. He's at the Savoy."

I liked that. I liked that a lot. I said: "Thanks. Anything else?"

Glyder said: "Yes. You had a drink, according to what you told the Old Man, at Charles' Bar in Paris. That was soon after Jane called at your apartment there. He said you'd told him there was another man present—a man called Marcini. He said also that according to your description of this man it might be a certain Czech called Salosis, and if it was, Salosis was somebody you might keep an eye on if you come across him again."

"O.K. It looks as if the Old Man's been working overtime."

Glyder said: "He's certainly showing interest. Can I have another drink?"

I nodded. He went to the sideboard and refilled his glass.

I said: "Now you're here, perhaps you'd like to do something for me. The situation is briefly this: Sonia Karakoff—the woman we were talking about yesterday—is going to turn herself into a person called Sabina. She's going to front for her. We don't know who Sabina is or where she is. We're taking a chance, see?"

He said: "I see..."

I went on: "Sonia Karakoff is going to call at the flat of a Madame Olga Volanski, who's over here and says she's a White Russian. She might be. She might not be. I'm going to arrange with Karakoff and she's going round to Volanski's flat to-morrow night. The flat is in St. John's Wood. I'll give you the address. I want a tail put on Karakoff—not because I distrust her, because we know all about her and she's all right, but I wouldn't like anything to happen to her, see?"

"You mean she ought to come away again. How long will the interview last?" asked Glyder.

"I don't know," I said. "But I suggest when she does come out you might call me on the telephone."

Glyder said: "All right. Anything else?"

I shook my head. "There's nothing else. But the next time you see the Old Man, if you see him before I do, you might tell him I think I've got the explanation about Madame St. Philippe. That's the lot."

Glyder said: "No. There's just one other little thing. The Old Man asked me to give you this. He said nothing more. Just to give you this."

He handed me a piece of paper. Written on it, in the Old Man's straggling handwriting was:

Miss Valerie Rockhurst,
Valley House,
Near Balcombe,
Sussex.

I thought the Old Man wasn't so bad. From time to

 Peter Cheyney

time he threw something into the kitty—like this address. Usually, when you asked him a direct question or for a definite instruction he would evade the subject or change it. He could be maddening. But, and I'd always had to admit it, there was method in his madness.

I thought it was time I went to see Miss Rockhurst. After which she'd either do something or she wouldn't. Actually, I didn't quite see what she could do.

I said: "Have you got a stooge working for you, Glyder? Someone intelligent."

He thought for a moment. "There's Greeley," he said. "Horace Greeley. Do you remember him?"

I told him I did. I went on: "There's a dress shop in Mayfair... Bruton Street. It's called 'Yvette Cambeau.' Tell Greeley to be around there from eight o'clock onwards to-night. I want to know who goes in and out, and anything else that he can pick up. Let him stay on there until midnight and then telephone me and I'll give him some further instructions."

He finished his drink. He said: "All right. Well, so long. Good hunting and happy landings, if you want a nice mixed metaphor."

He went away.

I drank another cup of tea and smoked a cigarette. Then I put on my hat; went out; picked up a cab and drove to the Savoy.

Janey, I discovered, had a suite on the first floor. They telephoned through to him. Going up in the lift I wondered what our interview would bring forth. But I'd made up my mind that unless he had something very good to say I was going to make things hot for him.

He looked the same as usual—cool, calm, collected and very well-dressed. He showed little surprise at seeing me.

He said: "It's funny that you should turn up. But the world's a small place, isn't it?"

I said: "It's either too large or too small. Never the right size! I want to talk to you."

"All right. Talk..." He grinned at me. "Is there anything to stop you?"

"No..." I went on: "I don't know you very well, Janey. I've just come across you half a dozen times in Frankfurt and in Paris. You remember the afternoon that Olly was killed?"

"Yes, I remember. You told me about him."

I said: "You didn't kill him by any chance, did you?"

He looked at me for a long time. "What the hell do you mean?"

I said: "Work it out. That afternoon I had an appointment with Olly in one of the side streets off the Faubourg St. Honoré. All I found was his beret. So I had a look round, and parked quite close to this spot was the car you were driving—a 6/15 Citroen. I looked at the number plate. It was rather peculiar. Somebody had painted the number of the car you were driving in Frankfurt over Rockie's number. They'd done it very badly, too. It struck me as being rather odd that you should be driving Rockie's car, because you may or may not know that he's disappeared, and I think the Russians have got him. Because—and I'm not even going to ask you to keep quiet about this; it will go very badly with you if you talk—Rockie wasn't what he seemed to be.

                                     Peter Cheyney

He wasn't just the stupid, too rich play-boy. He was a very astute agent of the secret service of this country. So you can imagine I was rather surprised when I realised that you were driving his car, and it's my bet that that was the car that killed Olly. It was too much of a coincidence that that car should have been almost at the spot of his death."

He began to speak, but I stopped him.

"Just a minute. It was also a coincidence," I went on, "that sometime before Olly was killed in the afternoon, that car was driven into my garage in Paris. It was refuelled and the tyres were checked. There was a note about this in Olly's day-book. I went back to the garage and checked this myself after I left you. The presumption is that you know a great deal more than you've told me. Incidentally, why did you come round that afternoon to see me? And why when I asked you in Charles' Bar how you got my address did you say that you'd got it from the hall porter at The Travellers' Club in Paris? I checked on that, too. You didn't. Now do some talking."

He spread his hands. He said: "I suppose you've some sort of right to ask these questions?"

I nodded. "You'll find that out. You'll find that out if I'm not satisfied with what you have to say. We still have the War Emergency Act operating here and that's as good as anything else to pinch you under, Jancy."

He grinned: "I'm not worrying. But all this is very amusing, and a little bit frightening, although I think it's much more innocent than you think. The day before I left Frankfurt for Paris I smashed my car up. I was in the bar there at the Grand Hotel. I was grousing about the car, and a rather extraordinary thing happened—except it wasn't perhaps so extraordinary. There was a woman in the bar—a tall, very attractive woman, dressed in black. She said if I wanted a car she'd lend me one. She wanted the car driven to Paris and left there. She asked me if I'd like to have it and garage it in Paris.

"That was how I got the Citroen. I didn't know it was Rockie's car. Why should I? She said it might be a good idea to put mycar number on the plate because the car wasn't licensed under the number that was on it, and my own car was a Citroen so nobody would think anything of it." He shrugged his shoulders. "I'd have done anything to get a car, so it seemed reasonable.

"The car was parked in a garage nearby. I had my own number put on it in case of accidents; drove down to Paris. It's quite right that when I arrived I went into a garage and filled up in the afternoon. I didn't know it was your garage. How should I? If Olly was there I wouldn't recognise him. All I knew was that you'd told me that you were running a garage and you'd told me you had an amusing old Frenchman as your foreman or manager."

He went on: "There was another thing. This woman who loaned me the car apparently knew about you. She asked me if I knew you and I told her I did. She said if I saw you in Paris to remember her to you. She was rather odd. She asked me to give you a message, and she asked me to give it to you just like this: She said: 'This is rather confidential but tell Kells that he ought to have written to me before. It's such a long time since I've heard from him; that he ought to know that I'm very impatient;

                                    Peter Cheyney

that ladies won't wait.'"

I got it. I said: "All right. You wouldn't know this lady's name, would you?"

"Of course. She gave it to me, so that you should know who the message came from. Her name was Hermione Martin."

I asked: "After you'd been to the garage, where did you leave the car?"

He said: "I left it in the Rue Royale. When I saw you in your apartment I didn't give you the message. I intended to tell you all about it whilst we were having a drink. We went to Charles' Bar. We hadn't been there a minute before Marcini came in. You remember the man? Naturally I said nothing. She'd told me that this business was confidential, and knowing you and your lady friends I thought I'd tell you about it when we were alone."

I asked: "What then?"

"When I went back to the Rue Royale to pick up the car it was gone. I didn't know what the hell to do. If I reported it to the police there was going to be trouble about the registration number. I decided to see you about it before I did anything."

"And then?" I asked.

He said: "I went back to your place the next day. You'd gone. You'd left no address, and I couldn't get in touch with you. Well, I'm telling you now."

He lighted a cigarette. "So Rockie was in the cloak and dagger brigade?"

"Yes," I said. "The operative word is 'was.'"

He looked at me. "And I suppose you are, too."

I said: "Right first time."

He rang the bell. He said: "It's a pity we didn't have this discussion before. Maybe it was my fault, but I didn't think it was all that important, you know."

"Why should you? If you're what you seem to be."

He said: "That's easily proved if you liked to have my passport and identification checked."

"Don't worry, Janey. We'll find out if what you say is true all right. If it isn't we'll have you."

He said smilingly: "I'll take the chance."

The manservant answered the bell. Janey said: "Bring some whisky and soda and ice...."

**I WAS** back at my flat at six o'clock. Things were beginning to take shape in my head. There was no doubt in my mind that the woman who'd lent Rockie's car to Janey in Frankfurt was the Old Man's missing agent Hermione Martin. There couldn't be any question about it. I thought it was tough luck on Hermione, and it was easy to see what she was trying to do. By some means or other she'd come across Rockie. For all I know she might have been working with him, and she knew how, when, and why he'd disappeared. Not only that; she'd got his car. Maybe Rockie had lent it to her. After which somebody got at him. He was killed or kidnapped—both processes being pretty normal in that part of the world. Also it was obvious that Hermione, whom I did not know, had heard about me. The Old Man had probably told her that I was at a fixed point in Paris; that if she got into any difficulties she was to get in touch with me. And this was a good way for her to do it. First of all she wanted to get rid of Rockie's car. This car was hot. The German police would be looking for it and the boyos who'd kidnapped or killed Rockie would be after it too. So she wished it on to Janey, but she got him to change the number first, cleverly. She didn't want the car to be recognised.

Then in case she failed to communicate with me in Paris, which she intended to do immediately, she told Janey to come and see me. She gave him that fake message with the Old Man's code word. She thought that that and the sight of a car which I would probably recognise as being Rockie's—because I'd driven it a dozen times—would at least put me on the alert. Having got rid of Janey she took the first plane she could and flew to Paris. Probably she was being chased at the time. Someone was after her.

When she arrived she waited around near Maxims so that she could indicate to me that she wanted to talk to me. She was afraid of doing this except in circumstances that I wanted. Then she made the appointment to meet me. And I bet she had plenty to say, too.

I thought it was tough luck on Hermione. There was no doubt about what had happened. Janey, who didn't know how wise he was being, cleverly did not give me the message in front of Marcini who was, as the Old Man had suggested, working on the other side, and who had listened in on my conversation with Janey at Charles' Bar, because he probably thought that Janey was in the game, too.

Martini tipped off the situation to some woman outside, who picked me up that night when I left my apartment, followed me round to the Place des Roses, and the rest is obvious. My guess was that I'd been followed from my apartment by the woman who'd killed Hermione Martin, alias Theodora St. Philippe. It was obvious too what she'd done. Hermione must have known plenty. She had to be stopped talking to me at all costs. I realised a little bitterly that if I'd gone straight into the house at the Place des Roses instead of wandering about and smoking a cigarette before I went in, she might still be alive. The woman who'd killed her had slipped into the house while I was walking about the cul-de-sac. She'd gone straight up to the apartment, knocked and entered on some excuse. She'd gone into the bedroom with Hermione and killed her. She'd slipped out of the side door. And that was that.

So there were two other people to look out for. One was Marcini, who was probably Salosis, the Czech the Old Man had talked about, and the other was the woman who had spoken to me from Hermione's bedroom—just after she'd killed her.

These two were still in action. They were probably in England. They'd stopped Hermione from talking and their next job would probably be to get me.

I thought it was time somebody did something about those two.

And I hoped it would be me.

                              Peter Cheyney

# VI. — MARCINI

**IT** was a hot, sunshiny day. I left the flat at half-past twelve; got out the Jaguar; drove to the Ritz. I parked the car, went into the hotel, lighted a cigarette and amused myself by walking up and down the long passage that led to the restaurant.

Five minutes afterwards, Sonia arrived. She looked superb. She was dressed in a tailored, coral-coloured linen coat and skirt; a plain black picture hat; black suede shoes and handbag.

She said: "I was thrilled when I got your telephone message this morning. So I am going to start doing something? I am excited."

"Maybe the excitement will wear off, Sabina. The thing is not to get too excited."

She said: "And I must not forget that I am Sabina."

"Don't... it might be a little tough for you..."

We went into the restaurant. When we were seated I said: "Tell me exactly who you are and what you have to do, because you are going to St. John's Wood to-night to see Madame Olga Volanski."

She said: "Tell me something, Michael. This woman Volanski—is she clever or is she a fool? Is she for us or is she against us? I would like to know something about her."

I said: "All I can tell you about her is that she is an old bag. She looks like hell. She is fat and unwieldy. Her face sags. She is over made-up. At one moment I think she is a very stupid woman; at another I think she may be a very good actress. It's your business to find out what she's like. Now tell me your story."

She rattled it off: "My name is Sabina. If there is any question about my second name I say that I have been using all sorts of names whilst I have been in England. I say that I take it that Madame Volanski may be considered as a friend and that I may talk quite openly to her because I know that she has been living with the man with whom I have been working—Colonel Riffenbach, late of the S.S. but known in this country as a White Russian—an ex-Hetman of Cossacks called Alexandrov. Therefore, because I know he was working for the Soviets, I know that Madame Volanski must also be sympathetic to their cause.

"I am terribly worried because Colonel Riffenbach has disappeared, but I am not very surprised at this because for some time it has been considered that he was not faithful to the U.S.S.R. He was captured by the Russians at the end of the war and he was given the choice of working for them or being sent to the Salt Mines. He elected to work for the Russians and whilst he had been entirely loyal for some years, he was—because that was the rule—never entirely trusted by his Chiefs. Therefore when he came to England on the secret business on which he was engaged, I—Sabina— was sent over here to make contact with him when he arrived, generally to give him his instructions and to see that they were carried out."

I said: "Very good. Go on..."

"It is obvious," Sonia continued, "that he has taken

  Peter Cheyney

the opportunity of being in this foreign country and of the money with which he has been supplied by me from time to time, to make his escape. Therefore, believing that Madame Volanski is sympathetic to our sacred Russian cause to bring about world-wide revolution, I have come to her to ask her to give me every bit of information available about him, and to find out if she can give me some clue as to his whereabouts. That is all I have to say."

"Very good, Sonia. That is excellent. All you can do is to try that and see how the old girl reacts. She may take your information in one of two ways. Either she is sympathetic with the Russians; she knew all about the so-called Alexandrov, in which case she is going to tell you the truth about everything and you may find out something more about this mysterious Sabina whom you are impersonating, and any other contacts which Riffenbach may have had in London or England. If, on the other hand, the old girl Volanski is, as she pretends to be, a White Russian, she is going to try to cause a hell of a lot of trouble for you with me. You'll have to look out for that. But in any case we shall know exactly where we are. Now, you arrive there to-night at eight o'clock."

I gave her a slip of paper with the address typewritten on it. "Arrive by taxicab, but stop it about fifty yards from the apartment house so that an operative of mine who will be watching can identify you and note the time that you go in and the entrance you use. That's all, and good luck to you."

She smiled at me. "I like very much to work with

you, Michael... very much indeed." She looked tenderly across the table.

I asked: "Why, Sonia?"

She looked at me for a long time. Then she said: "You know, Michael, I am strangely attracted to you. Always there must be some man in my life. I am sick of Rico. He is effeminate, and he also always lets me have my own way. He flies into rages and I hit him. It seems that I am always hitting him with bottles and throwing vases and things like that at him. He seems to like it and this does not appeal to me. I would prefer him to strike me or put me across his knee and give me a good beating. All Russian women like to be beaten by the men they love. Do you understand?"

I nodded. "I suppose so," I said. "What do you mean is that you believe that any man who really loved you wouldn't stand any nonsense from you?"

"Yes... yes." She gazed at me longingly. "That is why I like you, Michael. You have never tried to make love to me—which annoys me—and I think you are my type. I shall like very much working with you and then, when it is finished, I shall make you love me. Is that understood?"

I thought I wouldn't start anything at the moment with Sonia. Not until the job was finished.

I said: "Yes... I suppose so. But we'll do the job first."

She smiled, radiantly. "But lovely," she said. "So lovely. Now, please give me some champagne."

**IT** was about six-thirty when I drove the Jaguar through the entrance gates of Valley House. The

Georgian house, shaded by a fringe of trees and surrounded by parkland, stood some quarter of a mile
from the entrance gates, and I reflected rather sadly that
it was only possible for wealthy Americans and the Coal
Board to own such houses in England these days.

I braked the car to a standstill in the gravel courtyard
before the main doors; rang the bell. After a minute or
two the double doors were opened by a staid and aged
butler. I gave him my card.

I said: "I'd like to see Miss Valerie Rockhurst for a
few minutes if that's possible."

He asked: "Have you an appointment, sir?"

I shook my head.

He said: "Miss Rockhurst has a cocktail party at
the present moment. I don't think she will like to be
disturbed."

I said: "Give me my card."

He handed it back to me. I took the card; wrote underneath my name: "I would like to see you about your
brother." I gave it to him. I said: "Take that in to Miss
Rockhurst."

"Very well, sir. Will you wait in the hall."

I waited in the hall. It was a large, square hallway.
The furniture was distinguished and one or two big
oil paintings gazed mournfully at me from the walls.
It was a lovely evening and the sun came through the
large, stained-glass windows at the end of a wide passage
running into the hallway. A few minutes passed; then a
door at the end of the passage opened and a girl came
towards me into the hallway.

I've seen some pretty, beautiful and lovely women in

my life, but this one was the best of them all. She was about five feet seven inches in height. Her face was oval, with a complexion like milk. Her mouth and teeth were almost perfect and as she approached me I could see that her eyes were blue and sparkling. Perhaps the most striking thing about her was her hair. She was an ash-blonde—a real one—and her hair, caught back on one side under a tortoiseshell slide, formed a perfect frame for her face.

She said: "Mr. Kells, I am Valerie Rockhurst. This card says that you would like to see me about my brother. I am busy, but I could spare you a few minutes."

This struck me as being a little casual. I thought that it might have been possible for her to spare even more than a few minutes.

I nodded.

She said: "Will you come this way?" She took me into a room off the hallway—a long, book-lined room with french windows leading on to the lawn. The room was bathed in sunshine and there were bowls of flowers everywhere.

She motioned me to a chair; sat down herself. She said: "Well, Mr. Kells?"

I was a little bit surprised. I thought that I should get more of a reaction from the Valerie Rockhurst who was so passionately fond of her brother; so devoted to him.

I said: "Miss Rockhurst, I want to ask you a few questions, but first of all I should like to talk to you about your brother. Had you any idea what he was doing in Germany; what his real job was?"

She raised her eyebrows. It struck me that she was

the most cool and collected person I had ever met.

"His real job, Mr. Kells? I never knew that he did any work. I always thought Rockie spent most of his life amusing himself..." she smiled—"sometimes in rather dangerous ways I am afraid— driving racing cars, flying aeroplanes, doing all sorts of things. I never regarded those things as work."

I said: "I didn't mean that, but in any event you've answered my question. So I think I'd better be quite candid with you, Miss Rockhurst. Your brother was, under that camouflage of a sporting play-boy, one of the most astute, courageous and determined agents in the employ of a branch of British Secret Service."

She said: "Really, Mr. Kells. You amaze me. I should never have suspected anything like that. And I wonder why Rockie should have elected to work for the British. One would have thought that if he'd wanted to do work of that sort he would have done it in one of our own American services."

I shrugged my shoulders. "I can't tell you anything about that. He made his own choice. And that was what he was doing when he disappeared not so long ago. I believe you were very concerned about that."

She said: "Naturally. I was very, very fond of my brother. I worried greatly about this business. Do you know what happened to him?"

I shook my head. "No. Tell me... what steps did you take about your brother's disappearance when it became known to you? I believe you were in Frankfurt at the time."

She nodded. "I went to the police. I went to the

British authorities. Eventually, I saw an officer—I think he was a member of an Army Intelligence Service. There was nothing else I could do. I stayed on for a week or two expecting to get some news. There was none. Then I came back here. At first, for a little while, I thought that Rockie had gone off on some jaunt. He used to do things like that, you know; disappear suddenly; then turn up a few weeks afterwards. I thought perhaps this was just another of those things."

I said: "I'm sorry to tell you I think it was a little more serious. I think Rockie, in the course of his business as an agent, fell into the hands of the Russians."

She said: "I see..." She paused; then: "Do I take it you are doing the same sort of work, Mr. Kells?"

I nodded. "If you want any verification of what I say, Miss Rockhurst, it can be in your hands in a few hours. In the meantime I'll be glad if you'll believe me. I think that your brother isn't dead."

"Do you?" she asked. "I wonder why you think that. I've often heard that people who disappear in the circumstances you have mentioned never come back."

"That's true," I said. "If the Russians know they are working for Allied Intelligence Services they usually have a very short way with them. They are either shot or what is even worse go to the Salt Mines."

She said: "I see... And you don't believe that Rockie is dead?"

I said: "No."

She asked: "Why?"

I said: "For one thing, a British agent working in Germany, who had many times been inside the Russian

                                        Peter Cheyney

Sector somehow became possessed of Rockie's car—the Citroen. She met a man I knew, whose car had been damaged, in Frankfurt. She lent Rockie's Citroen to him and made a special point of asking him to let me see the car. I was then in Paris. She knew, of course, that I would recognise it as Rockie's car which I had driven many times. She also sent a message which indicated that she herself was an agent. There was only one reason why she wanted me to see the car and that was to remind me of Rockie; to give me an indication that something was still afoot. You realise she wouldn't have bothered to send that car down to Paris if Rockie had been dead. Therefore, I took it that she had some knowledge of what had happened to him; that he was still alive."

She asked: "Did you see this woman?"

"I saw her," I said. "Unfortunately I hadn't the chance to speak to her. I managed to make an appointment with her. When I arrived at her apartment she was dead. She had been murdered."

She said slowly: "How awful. Why?"

"For one obvious reason," I told her. "It's my belief that she had important information about the whereabouts of Rockie. She had something very important to tell me, and our friends on the other side had made up their minds that she wasn't going to talk—that's all. I wonder if there is anything you could tell me—any remote thing that you remember about Rockie that would help me. Obviously, he never told you about what he was doing."

She said: "No. And I don't see that I can help you

very much, Mr. Kells, much as I would like to."

I said: "Miss Rockhurst, forgive me for saying this, but it struck me that you seemed almost disinterested in what has happened to Rockie."

There was another pause; then she said: "You know, Mr. Kells, I suppose in my heart I'm a fatalist. I was very fond of Rockie. I think he was a marvellous man and a wonderful brother. But what is there I can do? I am amazed at hearing your story to-day. But I don't think there is anything I can say or do that would help. Except one thing..."

"Yes?" I was interested.

She said: "Supposing for the sake of argument, as you suggest, that my brother is still alive, don't you think it might be a good thing to leave things as they are? If the Russians have decided not to kill him; if he's alive and kept there, isn't there a probability that he might escape? Rockie is very tough and clever. I think I'd back him to get out of any dangerous situation."

I smiled at her. "You don't know the Russians, Miss Rockhurst. If they're keeping him it isn't because they are concerned about his health. It means they're keeping him because they think he's got some definite information. If you read your newspapers you may have learned that they have rather peculiar means of separating agents from such information as they possess. These means are never very pleasant. Do you realise that?"

She nodded her lovely head. "I realise it only too well, Mr. Kells. But don't you think that interference on the part of the secret service in this country might cause him to be killed immediately?"

I said: "One's got to take a chance on that. You don't think it would be a good idea to leave him there, do you?"

She said: "I've said that Rockie is courageous and intelligent. It's quite on the cards that he might find his own way out of this."

"Is it?" I queried. "I wonder what gives you that point of view, Miss Rockhurst. You seem to stress it?"

She shrugged her shoulders. "I've no reason for saying that except that I believe in my brother."

I said: "So there's no way you can help me... nothing at all? There was nothing about his behaviour in Frankfurt and other parts of Germany that you visited which might give you some sort of clue as to what was in his mind? He never mentioned, I suppose, some place he was going to in the future; some odd remark which you might remember that might give us at least some clue as to what was in his mind?"

"No..." She stood up—a sign that the interview was at an end.

I got to my feet. Somehow I was entirely dissatisfied with my talk with her. She gave me the impression of beautiful aloofness; of disinterest. I thought it was amazing that a woman who was so fond of her brother should not even want to help.

I said: "I wonder if I might ask a favour of you. Could I see Rockie's room? He used to live here, didn't he, when he was in England? I should tell you that I was one of his best friends. We've known each other for years and we've done several quite dangerous jobs together. We liked and trusted each other."

She said slowly: "Why not?" She walked to the fire-place; rang a bell. After a few moments the butler came in. She said: "James, would you take Mr. Kells to Mr. Rockhurst's room? He wants to see it."

She held out her hand. "Good-bye, Mr. Kells. Whatever you do, I hope you will be lucky. Now, please excuse me. I must go back to my guests."

I stood there looking at the door. I thought that Miss Valerie Rockhurst was definitely a problem—quite an enigmatic one. In my mind I would have bet all the tea in China that she knew something but for some reason best known to herself she'd decided not to talk.

The butler said: "Will you come this way, sir?"

I followed him along the passage into the hallway and up the wide, curving stairs. We arrived at the first floor. He threw open the door of a room and said: "This was Mr. Rockhurst's room, sir."

I passed him; went into the room. It was the sort of room that Rockie would have. There was a large, antique, canopied bed. All round the room were trophies of his physical prowess. Two sets of golf clubs leaned against the wall in a corner. There was a collection of spears, rifles, pistols and automatics on a shelf over the mantelpiece. In the corner was a solitary small set of bookshelves filled with books. There couldn't have been more than thirty or forty books in the shelves. I recollected with a grin that Rockie hadn't spent much of his time reading, except the sporting news.

Somewhere in the house a bell rang. The butler said: "Would you excuse me, sir? I am needed downstairs."

I said: "Of course. I can find my own way down. I'd

like to stay here for a few minutes if you don't mind."

"Of course, sir." He went away.

I began to nose about the room. I didn't know what I was looking for and therefore I realised with a grin that even if I saw it I shouldn't recognise it. I walked over to the bookshelves and began to look at the titles of the books. I was attracted by one in the middle shelf. It was called This Is The Place. I took it out. By the jacket it was evidently some sort of tourist guide. I scanned through the pages. I was about to put it back again when I saw that, at the back of the space vacated by the book, the colour of the woodwork was not the same as that of the panelling on the walls. Very quickly I removed half a dozen more books. Then I saw a knob at the back of the bookcase. I pulled it. A small door opened on a hinge. Behind was a dark recess about a foot square. I took out my lighter; snapped on the flame; put it into the recess. Packed neatly in the recess were two or three dozen pass-port books. I took them out. Some of them were blank; some of them were filled in with a dozen or so of the names that Rockie had used on different occasions, be-cause his photograph was on each one. Jumbled against the wall was a collection of different coloured inking pads and rubber stamps. I grinned to myself. With his usual forethought Rockie had supplied himself with the means of faking any passport he wanted to.

I scanned through them quickly. Eleven of them were filled in and there were twenty-two blank ones. In addition there were steamer entrance and exit tickets. All the wherewithal to get in and out of most countries. I put the things back; closed the recess; replaced the books. I was not at all surprised at finding them. They were part of any agent's stock-in-trade; yet for some reason these things had a peculiar unsettling effect on my mind.

I walked back to the doorway. With those blank passports, stamps and other documents, practically anybody in the house with a little ingenuity had at close hand the means of getting out of England and getting into most European countries fairly easily, supposing they knew their way about. I wondered if anybody else in the house had knowledge of this passport recess.

I went slowly down the stairway. James, the butler, was waiting in the hallway. I crossed the hall. He opened the front door. I went out.

I drove the car back to London. I felt a definite surprise at the attitude of Rockie's sister. If you know what I mean, it didn't match up with her general appearance; what I'd heard about her. She was certainly a peach. I thought she was the most alluring thing I'd ever seen in my life. I thought, with more than a certain amount of self-interest, that I would very much like to see Valerie Rockhurst again. I made up my mind I was going to.

**IT** was nine o'clock when Glyder telephoned.

He said: "Look, Mike, how long do I have to wait outside this place? I'm talking to you from a call-box opposite the house. What time is the girl friend supposed to come out?"

I asked: "What time did she arrive, Glyder?"

He said: "About five minutes to eight. She stopped her cab down the road. I recognised her from the

                                    Peter Cheyney

description you'd given me. She went into the front entrance at eight. I haven't seen her since."

I saw no reason why Sonia should have been at Madame Volanski's apartment more than half an hour or three-quarters at the most.

I said to Glyder: "Go over there and go up to the second floor. You want the apartment of Madame Volanski. Ring the bell and say you've called to pick up Madame Sabina. See what you can find out."

He said: "O.K. I'll ring you back when I know—in a few minutes."

I lighted a cigarette; began to walk up and down my sitting- room. Maybe, I thought, I was worrying a little too much about Sonia. I didn't expect that she'd come to any harm at Madame Volanski's hands, and I didn't know anybody else who'd be particularly interested in her at the moment.

Five or six minutes elapsed; then Glyder came through again. He said: "She left there at a quarter to nine. She went out of the back way. The old bag Volanski said that whilst the girl was there she received a mysterious telephone call. The caller didn't give a name but said that Madame Sabina was in great danger and should leave at once—by the back way. She says she took her down; saw her out of the back entrance. This leads into a garden belonging to the apartment block. There is a path to the side gate which leads out on to the main road. Volanski says she saw no one else in the garden. Where do I go from here?"

"Just a moment," I said. "Do you think that Volanski is telling the truth?"

"You bet," said Glyder. "She's scared stiff. You could almost hear her knees knocking together."

I thought for a moment; then I said: "You'd better jump a cab and get back here immediately. Stop the cab at the garage and bring my car round."

He said: "O.K., Mike..." and rang off.

I wondered what could have happened to Sonia. It would be unlike her to go off anywhere or do anything on her own without reporting to me on her interview with Olga Volanski. And who the hell was this mysterious telephone caller who knew that Sonia was in the flat? Perhaps Sonia knew. Maybe she'd seen something or somebody on her way in—someone who had scared her—someone she thought might be waiting for her. It could be that. On the other hand, I might have been wrong about Madame Volanski and she might have had somebody posted out at the back entrance to fix Sonia.

I waited impatiently until Glyder arrived. He asked: "What goes?"

I said: "You know as much as I do. But we must also remember that Sonia was a newcomer in this game. She's been out of the business for a long time. So it rather points to Volanski and any friends she may have."

He said: "So you think Volanski has tipped the wink to somebody that Sonia was coming to see her and they've knocked her off."

I said: "It looks like that."

He asked: "Are you going to do anything about this Volanski?"

I said: "Why worry? It's Sonia I'm thinking about. Volanski has no passport. We can pick her up any time.

She's an old woman and can't move very fast. Anyway, where can she go? Come on."

I put my Luger into my pocket and we went downstairs; got into the car. I drove towards Fulham, threading my way through the evening traffic as quickly as I could.

Glyder asked: "What's the idea, Mike?"

I said: "The idea is the house near Forest Hills where you dealt with what was left of Riffenbach. Volanski doesn't know that I know of this house. If they wanted to take Sonia somewhere and work on her they'd take her there."

He said: "Which means that Riffenbach has other people who worked for him?"

"Maybe," I said.

I drove quickly but it was nearly twenty-past ten before we got to Forest Hills. I drove down the road towards the little white house; parked the car some distance away under a clump of trees.

I said to Glyder: "We separate here. Work towards the back of the house." I pointed to it in the moonlight. "Meet me somewhere round the back. We'll go in through the kitchen door."

We separated. I made my way across the fields, keeping in the shadow of hedges. After a few minutes I arrived behind the house. I could see no sign of a light, but the curtains were drawn. Glyder joined me. We made our way carefully through the white-painted fence towards the kitchen door. I tried it. It was unlocked.

I took out the Luger; quietly opened the door. I whispered to Glyder to keep behind me. We went into the passageway which had led to the room where I'd found Riffenbach. On the other side of the passage, almost opposite the sitting-room door, I saw a crack of light under a door. I stepped back; kicked the door open. We went in.

Glyder said: "Well... well... well..."

Sonia, looking delightful in a black lace dinner frock, was seated in a chair. Both her wrists were tied to one arm of the chair. On one side of the room was a ladder leaning up against the wall and tied to the top of the ladder was a wooden arm. Suspended from it was a large petrol tin.

Standing half-way up the ladder, fixing this strange apparatus, was Marcini. His head turned round with a jerk as he heard Glyder's voice.

I said: "Well, if it isn't my old friend Marcini. Come down. Keep your hands up or I'll give it to you." I said to Glyder: "Go over him. He's probably got a pistol somewhere. When you've done that, cut Sonia loose."

I said to her: "How are you feeling, babe? Have you had a nice evening?"

She said: "It is being a little better now, my dear Michael. Up to now it has not been fearfully interesting, and I am very glad you have arrived. You see what he is doing?"

I looked at the apparatus on the ladder. I said: "It looks like the Chinese water torture to me. Was that intended for you, my dear?"

She nodded. "He was going to make me talk. I don't know what he wanted me to talk about, but he said I was going to tell him what he wanted to know. He said it would take about twenty minutes of that to loosen my tongue."

Glyder went over Marcini. He said: "He has nothing on him."

I told Marcini to go and stand against the wall and to put his hands flat against it beside him. He did this. He said in his peculiar, rather high-pitched voice: "What do you think you are going to get away with? Do you think you are going to make metalk?"

I said: "I wouldn't mind betting that I'd make you talk if I wanted to, but I don't think anything you had to say would interest me very much. I think I can guess even where you got your instructions to pick up the girl friend here to-night. I expect he was waiting in the back garden for you, wasn't he, Sonia?"

She nodded. "Just before I got to the gate he was behind a tree. He came out behind me. He put a chloroform pad on my nose." She sighed. "I can still taste the stuff now. And as a perfume I don't like it. I prefer my own."

I said to Marcini: "I expect you got your instructions from someone in the Bruton Street shop, Marcini. Would you like to tell us about it?"

He shrugged his shoulders; gave me a peculiar half-smile. I thought he certainly had his nerve.

He said: "I'm not going to say anything, Kells. What can you do? This is England. I have been here before, you know. I don't think that you are going to do anything very tough. This is a free democracy, isn't it?" He was grinning.

Glyder went up to him. He said: "You know, you're

not a very nice-looking fellow, especially when you smile. Don't smile again." He slapped Marcini across the face—hard.

Marcini shrugged his shoulders again. He said: "Whatever you do I'm not going to talk."

Glyder looked at me and grinned. He asked: "Do you believe him? Do you want him to talk, Mike? Why don't we use his own water torture on him?"

I said: "It doesn't matter. I don't think he knows anything. Like Riffenbach, he was merely employed as a hewer of wood and a drawer of water. Riffenbach was a killer. So is this fellow." I said to him: "You followed me home after I went out of Charles' Bar in Paris. You had some woman working with you. She came after me when I went to see Madame St. Philippe. She killed Madame St. Philippe, didn't she?"

He said: "I don't know what you are talking about. You don't interest me. I'm not going to say anything whatever you do."

Marcini annoyed me, but I recognised the type. He was a tough, communist fanatic steeped in the insidious poison of that belief. He probably would be tough but there is a time when every man breaks down.

I said to Glyder: "See if the tin can's working."

Glyder went up the ladder. At the bottom of the tin can a little wooden stop was inserted. He pulled it out. He knocked the can with his hand. The water began to drip.

I said: "All right, Marcini. We'll soften you up a bit. I think an hour or so of that will make you a little more amenable to reason. Tie him to the ladder, Glyder."

   Peter Cheyney

Glyder said: "Come on. Come over here—or do I hurt you first?"

"I'm not coming," said Marcini. "And damn the pair of you." He put his hand to his mouth as Glyder jumped for him. Glyder was too late. Marcini stood against the wall grinning wickedly. He said: "You're not going to do anything to me and I'm not going to talk." His knees gave way and he fell on the floor on his face.

Glyder said: "He was ready for everything, this boyo. He's killed himself."

Sonia said in a tired voice. "It's most annoying. How I would have liked to see him under that tin can. They tell me that a couple of hours of that and one goes mad. That is what he was going to do to me."

I said: "Well, sweetheart, he hasn't done it, has he?" I put the pistol away; lighted a cigarette. I asked Sonia: "How did he get you down here?"

She said: "We came down by car. I was very dazed, but I had to walk a little way, so I expect he's left it somewhere near this place."

I said to Glyder: "Go and find the car."

"O.K., Mike." He went away.

I said to Sonia: "If I remember rightly, there's some liquor in this house in the room on the other side of the passage. Would you like a drink?"

She sighed. "Better than anything in the world would I like a drink. I'm so glad you got here when you did, Michael—otherwise that water business would have disarranged my coiffure."

We went across the passage. Riffenbach's bottles and glasses were still where I'd last seen them, except they were a little dustier. I cleaned up a couple of glasses with my handkerchief. We drank some brandy.

Glyder came back after five minutes. "There is a pathway about fifty yards away," he said, "leading off the road. There is a shed at the end of it, and the car was in the shed."

"What car was it?" I asked.

"A foreign car," he said. "An Opel."

I said: "It looks as if he came in as an ordinary citizen and brought his car with him. Go over him, Glyder, and see if there is anything on him."

When he came back, he said: "There's nothing. There are no tailor's tabs or marks on his underclothes." He grinned at me. "You didn't expect to find anything, did you?"

I shook my head. "Let's get him into the car."

We went back and picked up Marcini. We took him out through the back door; carried him to where the car stood in the open- doored shed. We put him in the driving seat.

I said: "Listen, Glyder, if this fellow had a smash in the car and he's found dead, no one's going to examine him—not for poison, are they? The road from here into the Forest Hills intersection is deserted."

He said: "I see."

I got into the passenger seat; switched on the ignition. I leaned across the inanimate body of Marcini; took the steering wheel. The car moved slowly down the path. When we came on to the secondary road leading towards Forest Hills, I took a look each way. There was nothing in sight. I listened. I could hear no sign of any

                                         Peter Cheyney

vehicle. I put my foot down on the accelerator and we moved forward. After three hundred yards we were doing about sixty. I opened the door; paused for a moment on the running-board; then jumped for the grass verge at the side of the road. I came down with a nasty jerk; then I sat up and looked at the car. It careered wildly along for about sixty yards; swerved; went into the ditch and turned over. There was a moment's pause; then the car did what I hoped it was going to do. It burst into flames.

I pushed my way through the hedge and began walking back towards the little white house.

**I**T was a quarter to twelve when we got back to the apartment. I produced a bottle of whisky and some glasses. We had a drink.

Sonia said: "This has been most interesting, Michael. What is the next thing I have to do? Maybe there are some more people who want to try and torture me and get information which I would not possibly give—because I do not know anything." She smiled at me.

I said: "You've done your job, my sweet. A very good one, too. I have found out all I wanted to know through your efforts and I am going to suggest that my friend here drives you back to your Yellow Penguin, where you can sleep in peace."

She looked surprised. "You mean I am finished?"

I said: "Yes, you are finished, Sonia, for the time being. I'll come down and see you one day next week. If I can, maybe I'll have a little memento—something you can wear in memory of to-night."

Her eyes brightened. She said: "I'd like that very much, Michael."

Glyder asked: "Will you want me again to-night?"

I said: "No. Look in and see me sometime to-morrow morning. I'll talk to you then."

They went off.

I lighted a cigarette; sat down in the arm-chair; put my feet on the mantelpiece. I sat there smoking, ruminating on the events of the day. I thought that the pieces of the jig-saw puzzle were beginning to fit in.

At twelve o'clock the telephone rang. It was Horace Greeley.

He said: "Is that you, Mr. Kells? Glyder said I was to ring you at midnight. I've been on this Bruton Street shop. About twenty minutes ago a woman arrived here in a car. She got out of it under a street lamp and is she a looker or is she!"

I said: "Tell me something, Greeley. Is she fairly tall, with a good figure? Has she got the most marvellous ash-blonde hair?"

Greeley said: "Right first time, Mr. Kells. What do I do?"

I said: "Wait till she comes out and then go after her. I expect you have a car, haven't you?"

He said: "Yes, I've got the Morris two-seater in a mews round here."

I said: "Go after her. Go after her car until she gets on to the Balcombe road in Sussex. If she takes the road that leads through the village you can come back. Telephone me at eleven o'clock in the morning. Good night, Greeley."

                               Peter Cheyney

He said: "Good night."
I got up, stretched and went to bed.

# VII. — MUSETTE

**I GOT** up at seven-thirty in the morning, drank some coffee and thought. I thought for a long time but nothing in this rather extraordinary business seemed to add up—not the way I liked things to add up anyway. I had an idea at the back of my head that the Old Man was playing some game of his own; issuing me with such information as he decided from time to time; letting me do all the donkey work which up to the moment had consisted mainly of running round in circles. But, if you understand me, the mainspring was missing. I had to find the answer to one question and that was what was activating the rather peculiar string of people who were engaged in the "affaire Rockie."

I went through them. First of all, in order of appearance of the characters in this strange tragedy or farce, was Rockie. Rockie had disappeared. My guess was that he had been taken to Eastern Germany or Russia. He might be dead and he might be alive. Then there was Jane. I believed Jane. His background and record were known. And I had no reason to doubt that what he had told me was the truth. Jane had become mixed up in the business by accident. First of all because he had known Rockie for some time and, secondly, because Hermione Martin had asked him to bring Rockie's car to Paris. On consideration I thought it lucky that he had been accidentally involved. Marcini had been put on his tail and Marcini's action in arranging for Hermione Martin to be killed had started this business as far as I was concerned.

I was sorry Marcini was dead because he must have known quite a lot. Quite obviously he had been on to the unfortunate Madame St. Philippe alias Hermione Martin in Frankfurt. He had known that she had got Jane to drive the car down. He had probably followed Jane down to Paris. Because Jane had driven the car down, Marcini believed that he was working for us. Therefore, when I appeared in Charles' Bar in Paris he included me in those against him. I suppose it was purely by chance that he tailed me back to my apartment and put in the woman who had followed me when I went round to see St. Philippe—the woman who quite obviously had killed her before she could talk to me. These were the Paris characters.

Then in England, we had first of all Madame Olga Volanski and, perhaps more importantly, Riffenbach. And Riffenbach gave me food for thought. He was working for the Russians all right. That was obvious. It was also obvious that he was not particularly trusted by them. Somebody—possibly Sabina; certainly not Madame Volanski, who I thought was a little too stupid to be really involved—was acting in a supervisory capacity, keeping her eye on Riffenbach. And for what?

Obviously to see that he carried out his job. So that if, for the sake of argument, Riffenbach was here to do a job but was not good enough to be trusted to do it on his own, then I imagine he was here in a purely bull-dog capacity. Remember his background. He had been a Commandant of a Concentration Camp—a job usually given to people distinguished for their cruelty. I was certain in my mind that Riffenbach had been over here in some strong-arm capacity.

But the key to the whole thing was Sabina. Sabina was the person whom I wanted to meet. I was certain that she was the head of the oufit working against us. As it was, I felt that I was running round in circles. I didn't know what these people were here for; what they wanted. If there was some connection between the operations of this gang in England and the disappearance of Rockie, nothing had emerged to show what it might be.

At eight o'clock I rang through to M.I.5 and asked for the use of an officer of that department for a couple of hours. I wanted somebody who could show a warrant card if necessary. In twenty minutes he arrived. He was a detective-sergeant who had done duty with the Special Branch and M.I.5—a nice-looking and intelligent fellow named Williamson.

We walked round to the garage, got out the Jaguar and I drove to St. John's Wood. I thought the sooner I had a little talk with Madame Volanski the better—if she was there. I thought she would be.

She was. We went straight up to her apartment and rang the bell. We rang it for a long time. Then she opened the door. She looked like the wreck of the Hesperus. She was bad enough when she had had time to titivate herself up, to dress carefully and to cake her face with that awful enamel. But, looking at her as she stood in the open doorway with only that surprised look on her face, I thought that nature in the raw was really never mild.

I said: "Good morning, Olga. Can we come in and talk to you?"

"But of course, my friend. I was going to telephone you this morning. I am miserable and so un'appy."

I asked: "Did you get drunk last night? Did you seek solace in vodka?"

She shook her head. "I was too frightened—much too frightened..." She led the way into the drawing-room. She asked: "Do you want a dreenk?"

I said: "Not at this time of the morning. But you have one. You'll probably feel better after it."

"Yes... I will dreenk just one..." She went to a sideboard cupboard; produced a bottle of vodka and a glass. She gave herself a tot; drank it off. When she turned towards us I could see that her eyes were brimming with tears.

I said: "Look, Olga, just forget to cry for once, will you? Exactly what happened last night, and why were you so frightened—or weren't you frightened?"

She said: "By God... I was frightened! This woman arrives just after eight o'clock. She arrives—this Sabina... God, is she a beech? I could tear her eyes out. I would like to keel her and spit on her grave."

I said: "That's fine. What did she have to say?"

"She 'ad a lot to say—too much for me. First of all this woman is Russian; this I guarantee. And she is pretty and she 'as, what you call it... sex appeal... and she knows 'ow to dress 'erself... and she is a lot younger than I am. Directly I saw 'er I thought to myself: My God... so this dirty Alexandrov, who is really some

German spy, is making love to this woman all the time and probably giving 'er presents which are bought with my money. This man 'as 'ad thousands from me. And what do I get?"

I said: "Did you tell her what you thought about her, Olga?"

She shook her head. "The damn woman never gave me the chance. Directly she gets inside the flat she starts to tell me an awful lot. She is making one mistake though. Of course she never thought she was going to 'ave to see me personally. So she makes the mistake of thinking that I am in this dirty affair with them. She does not realise that from the start I 'ave been tricked and deluded by this filthy Riffenbach; that I know nothing of their foul business."

"But you didn't tell her that," I asked.

"No, I did not tell her anything. She sits 'erself down and tells me all this. She tells me Riffenbach is working for the Russians. She tells me she is working with 'eem; that she is, in fact, 'is boss. She asks me all sorts of questions. She says that this Riffenbach 'as disappeared; that 'e cannot be found. She says that I must know something of 'is whereabouts; that 'e must 'ave told me something about 'is going off; where 'e was going to— such theengs like this. When I got the chance I told 'er I knew nothing about 'eem; that 'e 'as lied to me from the first; that I know nothing about 'is business; that I don' know where 'e 'as gone; that I don' care where 'e 'as gone; that I never want to see 'eem again in my life."

I nodded my head. I thought that Sonia had been pretty good and played her part very well. I asked:

  

"What then?"

She said: "She frightens me. She says that if I talk to anybody about what is 'appening, if I mention the name of Riffenbach to anybody; if I do anytheeng at all except keep my mouth shut, my life will not be worth twopence. This woman threatens she will 'ave me murdered—'ere in England—by Bolsheviks. Well..." She spread her hands. She looked at me pitifully—"so what 'appens to me? Am I going to be murdered in Piccadilly?"

I said: "You have some more vodka. Sit down. Take it from me, nobody's going to murder you, Olga. You're not valuable enough. You've served Riffenbach's purpose, and that's that."

She said: "Wait a meenute... somebody knew that this woman Sabina was coming 'ere..."

I pricked up my ears at this. "Why do you say that?"

"Because," she said, "while she is 'ere the telephone bell rings. I go away. I answer the telephone. Somebody says to me: 'You 'ave a young woman in your apartment?' I say: 'Yes.' They say: 'You will ask 'er to go out by the back door. You will tell 'er that she is in danger if she goes out by the front entrance. You will take 'er out secretly.'"

I said: "Yes, Olga, and what did you do about this?"

She said: "I wanted to get 'er out of my apartment. She frightened me—this woman. So I tell 'er somebody 'ad telephoned me and said she should go. I took er downstairs. I led 'er out into the garden. I showed 'er the path that leads to the gateway. She goes. That is all I know."

"Thanks, Olga. You've been very useful." I walked over to the window and looked out on to the quiet street below. Something was quite obvious. Nobody except me had known that Sonia was going to visit Olga Volanski, so someone had been keeping tabs on the front of the house—somebody who had been clever enough to keep themselves away from the quick eyes of Glyder. They had seen Sonia enter and had got in touch with Marcini, who had planted his car in the side street at the gate at the end of the pathway, and supplied himself with some chloroform to put Sonia out with. Quite obviously, somebody was very interested in anyone who came to visit Madame Volanski. They had made up their mind that this person was going to talk. Marcini, who was a hundred per cent tough and a hundred per cent for what he was doing, had picked up Sonia and had proposed to force the truth out of her. Well, where did we go from there?

I turned away from the window. I said: "Well, Olga, you're in a spot, aren't you? How much money have you got?"

She said: "I 'ave enough. I told you I 'ave money in America and I 'ave no doubt that some arrangement could be made 'ere to get some of it to me."

"That will have to wait for a bit," I told her. "Don't worry about this, but I am going to put you on ice for a bit, firstly for your own safety and secondly because Riffenbach having taken your passport with him, you are an alien in this country without a passport. Don't worry. What you're going to do is to stay quietly on here and I hope it won't inconvenience you very much

                                    Peter Cheyney

but you will have to report to this officer every morning. You go and see him at the address he will let you have. You just say good morning to him and totter off until the next morning. Don't worry about anybody killing you. This gentleman will have somebody keeping observation on this apartment. Nobody is going to get at you, Olga."

She said: "I see... Well, I am very glad I am not going to be murdered. How long does this 'ave to go on for?"

"I can't tell you," I said. "But I want to ask you one or two things. This dress shop in Bruton Street. You said at first it belonged to you. That isn't true, is it?"

"No. I told you that when I first talked to you because Riffenbach 'ad told me to say that. What 'appened was this. When we were in Paris 'e said it might be a very good thing for me to 'ave a business 'ere—a dress business. 'E said it would be something for me to do— something to amuse me. I gave 'eem some money—'alf a million francs. I don' know what 'e did with it. 'E said this business was doing well."

I asked: "Have you ever been there, Olga?"

She said: "Yes... I went there one day. 'E took me there. It is just an ordinary dress shop."

"Who was running it?" I asked.

She said: "There was a French girl there. She was a nice girl—pretty and chic—obviously a seller of clothes. I don' know what 'er full name was but 'er first name was Musette. There was a workroom there, and there were some girls working. I stayed there a little while and I went away. Afterwards I said to Riffenbach that I would like to 'ave some money from the shop. I needed money to buy some frocks. 'E laughed and said there would be an accounting at the end of a period, or quarter or something. Until then I must wait."

I said: "Thanks, Olga. I'll be seeing you soon, I hope. And don't forget to report to this gentleman—his name is Detective- Sergeant Williamson—each morning."

She said: "You know, Meester Kells, you make use of me to an extraordinary extent. What 'ave I to do—stay 'ere all day and look at my fingernails."

"You won't do that, Olga—not while the vodka lasts. Behave yourself. Maybe one of these fine days we'll be able to get you out of your trouble." I grinned at her. "If you hadn't imagined yourself in love with the ex-Cossack Riffenbach you'd have been much better off."

She said: "You theenk so? No woman is ever too old to fall in love. The trouble with me is when I fall in love it is with scoundrels."

I said: "So long, Olga..." signalled to Williamson. We went out. As I went through the doorway of her drawing-room I could see her making a bee-line for the sideboard and some more vodka.

**WE** got into the car and drove to Bruton Street. It was a quarter to nine when we arrived. The shop Yvette Cambeau was quite an attractive-looking affair, freshly painted. The blinds were still down and the front door locked. There was a mews at the side of the shop. We went down this; found a side door leading to the back of the shop. The mews was deserted. It took Williamson about two minutes to get the door open. We went in.

We found ourselves in a small courtyard. There was

                                    Peter Cheyney

a little flight of stairs leading up to the back door. The lock only needed a push. We went into a room which was obviously used as a store-room. Cardboard boxes of all sizes, shapes and description, bearing the name of the shop, were stacked against the walls. A passageway from this room led through an ante-room, curtained off for fittings, into the shop. There was an air of untidiness about the place. One or two of the models on which gowns were displayed were pushed against the walls. I had the idea that Yvette Cambeau had flown. It looked to me as if the gown business had served its purpose.

On one side of the passageway that led from the store-room was a flight of stairs. We went up these. There was a large room at the top of the stairs which had apparently been used as a manufactory for the gowns. Two or three frocks in the throes of alteration lay about the place. There was an open cash box, empty; the work tables.

I said to Williamson: "You can go back now. I shan't want you any more. Keep an eye on Volanski. Let her know where she is to report to you, and see that nobody gets her."

He said: "All right." He went away.

I went down into the shop; arranged the models to my own satisfaction; pulled up the blinds. I took the front door off the latch.

I sat down and waited for the post to arrive.

**IT** was just after nine o'clock when I thought I heard steps moving in the room above the shop. I went quickly and quietly up the stairs; pushed open the door of the room I had examined not long before—the workroom. Standing in the middle of the floor was a young woman.

She was of middle height; dark haired. She had a round, almost pretty face. She looked at me in amazement.

I said: "Good morning. Can I do anything for you?"

She spread her hands. "But, M'sieu..." she said. "I don't understand this. I work here. The girls should have started work half an hour ago. Nobody is here. Look... models and things are pushed all over the place...! What has happened?"

I asked: "What is your name, M'selle?"

"I am Musette. I am in charge of the workroom here. Also I am the fitter. The staff should arrive here at half-past eight in the morning. There are three girls who work here. Also about this time Madame should arrive."

I said: "And Madame... who is she?"

"Madame Yvette," she said. "The proprietor of the shop. It is most extraordinaire."

I said: "I wonder. Actually, Musette, I don't think you are going to see your proprietress any more. I think she has got out while the going was good."

She nodded her head slowly. "I see...! I thought there were some strange things happening lately. Perhaps it is money. And also I think the time is here when the rent is due. I don't think that Madame Yvette has been doing good business lately. Maybe she has what they call 'shot the moon.'"

I said: "Yes. I think you are right. I think she has. What was she—a Frenchwoman?"

                                    Peter Cheyney

She said: "M'sieu, would you tell me something? Are you from the police?"

I nodded. "As near as maybe. Anyway, I was very keen to have a few words with Madame Yvette Cambeau, who I believe was the proprietor of the business, and"—I continued—"if you didn't know she was leaving the place or going off or doing whatever she has done, how is it that the other girls—the work girls—haven't turned up?"

She shrugged her shoulders. "I don' know, M'sieu. Perhaps she got in touch with them; told them not to come; told them that the place was closing. But it is very strange she didn't tell me."

I asked: "Were you here yesterday?"

"Yes, of course. I was working here. I worked here until six o'clock."

I said: "Well, Musette, my guess is that she is not coming back. Do you know where she lived?"

She shook her head. "She lived somewhere in the West End, in an apartment block, I believe," she answered, "but I have never been there." She shrugged her shoulders again. "Always I had the idea that there was something rather extraordinary about this business—something peculiar. It didn't seem to me like a dressmakers. I always suspected that there was something wrong."

I said: "Well, now you know, don't you? Maybe she didn't tell you anything about it because she hoped you'd clear things up here."

"What is there for me to clear up, M'sieu? I work here for a salary and it looks as if I am not going to be paid this week." She sighed. "Well... c'est la vie...! And there are lots of other jobs in London for me." She picked up her handbag from the table.

I said: "Just a moment, Musette. Maybe we'll find Madame Cambeau. If we do I'll let you know. Would you like to give me your full name and address?"

She gave it to me—a number in Great Titchfield Street near Oxford Circus. I wrote it down.

She said: "If you find out anything, M'sieu, I would be glad to hear from you. I have not had my money for two weeks. Also I would like to tell Madame Cambeau what I think about her."

I said: "All right, Musette. I'll get in touch with you."

"Good morning, M'sieu..." She nodded brightly; tripped out of the room. I heard her footsteps descending the stairs.

I went back into the shop; lighted a cigarette and, through the plate glass window, watched Musette cross the road. She turned to the left and disappeared from my sight, a trim and not unattractive figure in spite of her lack of height. Then, from a small turning opposite the shop, I was very glad to see Williamson appear.

Obviously he had seen her hanging about before she came to the shop, had waited for her to make her exit and would tail her to wherever she was going. I was glad about this because I couldn't quite place Musette in my mind, and a little further information about her might help.

The nine o'clock post had arrived. Some envelopes had been pushed under the front door. I opened them. There were five altogether. Three contained invoices for goods delivered. One was a letter of complaint from a woman who didn't like the way her frock fitted her. The last one was merely a sheet of folded quarto type-writing paper enclosed in an unsealed envelope. Typed on the notepaper was an intimation that in addition to the other attractions at the Cossaque Restaurant, which included a balalaika orchestra and a Hungarian singer, the Brothers Zeus had been engaged by the manage-ment and would appear at twelve o'clock midnight each evening.

The envelope was addressed in longhand to Madame Yvette Cambeau and written in the top corner was: "If away please forward."

I put the envelope in my pocket. I failed to see—unless the Cossaque Restaurant was a club of which Madame Cambeau was a member—why anyone should have bothered to inform her of the appearance of the Brothers Zeus. The rest of the envelopes I put on the desk in the corner of the shop.

I picked up my hat; took a final look round. I walked back to my apartment.

I had a decided idea that the establishment known as "Yvette Cambeau" had closed for good.

**AT** eleven o'clock Greeley came through. He said: "I went after the ash-blonde last night, Mr. Kells. She went through Fulham, took the Eastbourne road, branched off towards Balcombe, ran through the village and turned into a big house called Valley House."

"Right, Greeley," I said. "Go out to Balcombe, and take it easy when you get there. I don't want anyone to recognise you or associate you with me. Get around the village and check up who is staying at Valley House. You'll get this from the tradesmen. Find out who the servants are who are employed there and where they come from. Pick up anything else you can. Telephone me when you've got some results."

I hung up the receiver as Glyder arrived.

I asked him: "What happened about Marcini? Is there anything in the newspapers?"

He nodded. "It's O.K. The local police officer found him in the early hours of the morning. They believe it to be a normal road accident. Apparently there was a steering defect in the car which, they think, caused it to run into the ditch and turn over. They're trying to get an identification of Marcini. The inquest is adjourned."

"I wish them luck," I said.

He helped himself to a drink—four fingers of whisky—and took it neat. I thought he must have a hell of a stomach to take it like that in the morning.

He sat down. He asked: "Where do we go from here, Mike?"

I shrugged my shoulders. "Your guess is as good as mine," I told him. "But we've got to get going somewhere or we'll have the Old Man on our necks."

"Maybe he knows something more than you do," said Glyder. "You know his habit of hanging out on everything until the last moment. Why don't you ask him?"

"And have my ears bitten off," I said. "If he wanted to talk he'd talk. Anything he knows is dependent on something I produce. See what I mean? If he's got something, he's holding out on it because it's depend-ent on some unknown factor which he expects me to produce."

I told him about my visit to "Yvette Cambeau," and of my talk with Musette.

He thought for a while, sipping his whisky. Then he said: "You know, Mike, this job looks to me like a double-cross. Somebody or other is taking somebody else for a ride."

I nodded. "I'm particularly interested in Riffenbach," I said. "Riffenbach was damned careless. Remember he took Carla out to the house at Forest Hills. That was stupid of him, wasn't it? This place is some sort of headquarters. Marcini knew of it. He took Sonia there. Sabina, who was apparently Riffenbach's boss or at least closely connected with him on this job, wrote her original letter to him—the one I found on his body—at that address. So the place is important to them. Yet Riffenbach, who was a dyed-in-the-wool operative, trained by the Russian Secret Service, was careless enough to take Carla out there. For all he knew, there was a chance that she might turn up some time at an inopportune moment. D'you get it?"

He shook his head. "No, I don't," he said.

"Riffenbach wasn't careless," I said. "He was a tough egg and would be loyal if it paid him. But he wasn't loy-al, and there was only one reason why he shouldn't be. He was planning to make a getaway from the Russians. And he was going to do it fairly quickly."

Glyder asked: "How do you work that one out?"

"Listen," I said. "It's obvious. He comes here via

Paris. And my guess is that Sabina was already waiting here in England for him. She was his boss because the Russians wouldn't trust him— even after years in their service—on his own. Sabina, I'll bet you any money you like, is Madame Yvette Cambeau, late of the Bruton Street shop. And there wasn't any affaire between Sabina and Riffenbach. The letter she wrote to him complaining that she hadn't seen him and that he was falling out of love with her was meant to indicate to him that he wasn't getting on with the job and that it was about time he got cracking. Riffenbach was careless enough to take Carla to the house in Forest Hills because he was all set to make a getaway. He'd succeeded in what he had planned. He had got out of Russia. He had picked up Olga Volanski and taken her for all the money she had, in addition to which he must also have received money from Sabina or some other Russian paymaster over here."

I lighted a cigarette. "That letter from Sabina," I went on, "was to tell him that she knew all about his affaire with Olga and to warn him to watch his step."

Glyder nodded. "Could be," he said.

"Now we have some more trouble," I told him. "We have the rather peculiar business of Rockie's sister. When I saw her I was particularly struck with what seemed her lack of interest in her brother's death. She didn't believe he was dead and she backed him to make a getaway. Which is goddam nonsense, anyhow. She knew as well as you or I know that people don't make getaways from the Russians. She was trying to stall me from going on with the business of finding out where he was and if he

                                      Peter Cheyney

was dead or alive."

"Very funny," said Glyder.

"You're telling me," I said. "She insinuates that it may be a damned bad thing for us to try and find her brother because if the Russians think we're after him they may kill him. Her attitude, for a girl who is supposed to be very fond of her brother, is just stupid."

"And then," I continued, "to cap it all, after my interview with her she goes dashing off to Bruton Street, that night, to interview—I suppose—Madame Yvette Cambeau. What the hell for?"

Glyder said: "It's a hell of a job, isn't it? And you've forgotten about Marcini. How the devil was he able to pick up Sonia when she went to see old Volanski? And he was prepared for the job."

I shrugged my shoulders. "There might be an explanation for that one. Remember the cocktail party to which I was invited. Well, there may have been other members of the organisation present at that party. I fell for the invitation and went, and this would enable any interested party to identify me. Maybe they told Marcini about me and he recognised me from the description they gave him. Maybe he wasn't waiting for Sonia. He was waiting for me and when he saw Sonia arrive he telephoned through to Bruton Street and said that I had not arrived but some girl was there. They might easily have told him to pick up the girl and find out who she was and what she was doing."

Glyder grinned. "It's your headache. But this Marcini was certainly something. He had the courage of his convictions all right."

"Marcini was a fanatic," I said. "He was one of those stupid people who delude themselves that what they are doing is right. And the fact that he poisoned himself rather than talk proves nothing. He'd been given a job to do and he had to do it. If he hadn't, he'd probably have come to a more sticky end than he did. These people mean business and they'll stop at nothing to get what they want."

Glyder grunted. "It's a pity we don't know what they do want. I know what I want. I want to go to Devonshire for a couple of weeks."

"Like hell you do," I said. "Here's what you can do. There's a club called The Cossaque—a night club— somewhere in Mayfair. You'd better see Woldingham or one of the Special Branch boys and find out what you can about it. If it's a respectable place arrange that you and I can go there to-night. I want to see a turn that's appearing about midnight. It ought to be easy for Woldingham to get hold of some members' tickets or, if he thinks it's better, an introduction from a member. It depends on the place."

Glyder got up. "O.K.," he said.

"Be here at a quarter to twelve," I told him. "And wear a dinner jacket. If you get yourself in the right frame of mind you'll probably find it will do you as much good as Devonshire."

He said: "Like hell...!" He went out.

I went into my bedroom, lay on the bed and closed my eyes. I was feeling pretty good and tired of the Rockie business. Something which had started as a more or less normal event—the disappearance of an agent—was

　　　　　　　　　　　　Peter Cheyney

becoming like a tin can tied to my tail. Wherever I went it followed me.

For some reason I began to think of Valerie Rockhurst—the mysterious lady whose motives I could not understand. It struck me suddenly that she seemed so sure that Rockie was alive that there was a possibility that she knew he was alive.

For a moment I played with the idea that the boyos who'd got Rockie had been to work on him properly. Everybody knows that their methods aren't exactly kid-glove. They've all sorts of methods—some of which never even leave a mark—of making people talk or see eye to eye with them. Maybe Rockie had broken under the strain and they were forcing Valerie Rockhurst—through him— to do something they wanted done over here. It could be.

But I'd lay all the tea in China against it. Rockie, I knew, would have killed himself somehow rather than spill any beans that he knew. And probably—under the Old Man's system—he knew damned little.

But whatever had happened the girl was playing some sort of game. Some game which she did not desire should be interfered with by people like myself sticking my nose into Rockie's disappearance.

I thought that one of these fine days I'd give myself the pleasure of a little straight talk with that young lady. I thought I might even get a little tough with her.

The telephone jangled.

It was Williamson. He said: "Mr. Kells, when I came out of the shop this morning a girl went in through the alley entrance. I didn't know what you'd want done, or if you'd seen her. So I waited and tailed her to an address in Great Titchfield Street. She came out soon afterwards and took a taxi somewhere or other. I've checked on her. Her name's Musette Lehaye and, apparently, she was the chief hand in the workshop at Yvette Cambeau. The landlady says she has a French passport and seems a very nice sort of girl."

"Good work, Williamson," I said. "By the way, do you know the time of the second postal delivery to-day in the Bruton Street area?"

Williamson said he thought it was four-thirty; that he would check on this.

"When you've checked on the time, be around Bruton Street when the post is delivered at the Yvette Cambeau shop," I told him. "I've an idea that the French girl Musette Lehaye may show up again to-day. Don't lose her when she leaves the shop whatever you do. Let me know what happens. Maybe her landlady will have a little more information for you later to-day."

He said he would take care of it.

I lay down on the bed and did a little more thinking. I was beginning to get a vestige of an idea in my head—an idea that had arrived from just nowhere at all, but which I found rather amusing and inspiring.

After all, you've got to work from something and even if that something is a false premise it provides a stepping-off place.

And I was fed up with the whole of this business. I couldn't break anything open. The Old Man wasn't talking—either because he didn't want to or because he couldn't. Nothing had come my way.

                                        Peter Cheyney

So now something was going to happen. Even if I
had to makeit happen.

Having made up my mind I went out to lunch on
the strength of it.

**I WENT** down Bruton Street about ten minutes past four. I entered the street from the Berkeley
Square end; strolled slowly down towards the shop. At
the far end of the street I could see Williamson leaning
up against a lamp-post reading a newspaper. I turned
into the little passageway by the side of the shop; opened
the side door with a skeleton key which I had put in my
pocket; went into the shop. The window blinds were up
and the shop door was locked as I had left it. The wax
models standing about in the window and on the shop
floor gave the place a weird air of unreality. I went out
into the passage, up the stairs and pushed open the door
of the workroom.

Musette Lehaye was sitting on a chair by the workta-
ble reading a French paper-backed novel.

I said: "Good afternoon, Musette."

She said quite calmly: "Good afternoon, M'sieu."
She got up; then sat down again. She turned down the
page of the book she was reading; closed it.

I asked: "What are you doing here, Musette?"

She shrugged her shoulders. "You understand,
M'sieu, I live in a room which is very nice to sleep in
but not good to stay in all day wondering about one's
next job. So I come here. I have been reading. You see,
Madame gave me the key to the side entrance because
often I arrived in the morning before she was here."

I offered her a cigarette. She shook her head. I lighted one for myself. I looked her over.

Musette Lehaye looked like what she said she was—a charge hand or forewoman in a dress shop. Her clothes were good but inexpensive, her shoes neat. She wore nylon stockings. Her hair was nicely done. Her face fascinated me. It was an ordinary, round, plain sort of face, but Musette's eyes were peculiar. There were deep shadows beneath them. I thought that somehow her eyes didn't match up with the rest of her appearance.

I sat down on the bench. I said: "So you came back to pass the time, Musette. Are you thinking of looking for another job?"

She shrugged her shoulders again; made a little moue. "I expect so, M'sieu. I shall have to do that in a day or two." She smiled suddenly. The smile illuminated her face. For a moment she looked almost pretty. She said: "Also the possibility occurred to me that Madame Cambeau might come back. It seems so stupid to go away and leave a shop like this with nobody in it. The shop door is locked. Customers may have been here for all I know. I thought there was a possibility that she might return. You will not forget, M'sieu, that I am owed two week's money."

I didn't say anything. I drew on my cigarette. She asked: "Does M'sieu wish to know anything else? Is there anything that I can tell him?"

I said: "Yes. Are you quite sure you came back here because you thought that Madame Cambeau might possibly be here? Is that it? How long have you been here, Musette?"

     

"About five or six minutes," she answered.

"Are you certain you didn't come to collect the afternoon post when it was delivered?"

She looked at me. Her eyes were wide. "Why should I wish to do that, M'sieu? What has the post to do with me? First of all, there is little post—an account or two—I have noticed that. But why should I be interested in the post?"

I said: "I don't know. I just wondered." There was a pause; then I went on: "Tell me about Madame Yvette Cambeau. What is she like? How does she dress?"

She thought for a moment. She said: "It is a little difficult to give exact details. When one looks at a person one gets an impression. But I think I can tell you. She is tall and very slim. She has a perfect figure—most excellent for our business. She has a pale, oval face and lots of dark brown hair which is always very well dressed. Her clothes are chic. She did not get them at this shop." She laughed and her face became pretty again. "Always she is very smart, but at the same time, M'sieu, I came to the conclusion that she is not what she seems to be."

I asked: "What does she seem to be, Musette?"

She said: "She is supposed to be a modiste from Paris, but I don't think she knows anything at all about France. I don't think she has ever been trained anywhere. She does not know where to buy things or what to do. Actually, most of the business here was arranged by me. I took measurements for such frocks as we made, and fitted them. I supervised the girls who were working here. There were three of them. Madame Yvette would come here sometimes a little late; stay for a few hours;

talk to a customer who came in. But always she would send for me."

I said: "Tell me, have you any idea at the back of your head, Musette, as to where she has gone? Do you find any explanation for this rather odd behaviour of being here one day and disappearing the next, leaving you with no instructions or wages?"

She thought for a moment; then she said: "M'sieu, just now you offered me a cigarette. Please, I would like one."

I gave her a cigarette; lighted it. She puffed at it with the air of a practised smoker.

She said: "You know, M'sieu, from the first I suspected something peculiar about Madame Yvette Cambeau. She speaks excellent French, and I do not believe she is a Frenchwoman. She has been to Paris... yes... maybe she lived there... but she is no Frenchwoman. That I know."

I asked: "What is she?"

She said: "I am certain she is a Russian. She looks like a Russian, you understand, M'sieu. You know that certain something a well-bred Russian woman always has—something that is different. Also once or twice I heard her humming to herself and she would sing a few lines of a song. When she sang, she sang in Russian. One of the girls who worked here—a girl we called Janette—was of Russian parentage. She also was certain that Madame is a Russian."

I asked: "Do you think she was a refugee?"

She nodded her head. "That is what I think," she said.

"And was there anything else you noticed, Musette?"

                                    Peter Cheyney

She said: "Yes, once or twice I suggested to her that I should return to the shop; that I should do some work up here in the evening. I suggested to her that stock models could be made very easily up here; that I was prepared to cut them out; that I could get the girls to work overtime so that it would be unnecessary to send our orders out. She would not have this. She told me that in no circumstances was I to return to the shop after I left, which was usually about half-past five in the afternoon. I think perhaps, M'sieu, that something went on here."

"What do you mean by that, Musette?" I asked.

She shrugged her shoulders. "I do not know, but I always had a feeling about Madame; that there was something strange—something dramatic—about her."

"A woman's instinct, hey? But you didn't come to any conclusions about these thoughts of yours? You hadn't any idea what was going on? How much used she to pay you, Musette?"

She said: "I had five pounds a week and a small commission on sales."

I asked: "What were the other girls paid?"

"Between three and four pounds a week, M'sieu," she said.

"So the running expenses of the shop must have been about twenty-five pounds a week," I told her. "Were you making anything like that in the shop?"

She shook her head. "One week we took only ten pounds. That is why I thought the thing was ridiculous. Also it seemed that Madame was not particularly keen on making money."

I said: "You think she had money. Was she rich?"

She shrugged her shoulders. "She must have had money. She used to arrive in taxicabs. She never walked anywhere. Once or twice when she went out to lunch, and expected someone to come to the shop, she would give me the phone number of the restaurant where she was lunching. Always expensive places, M'sieu."

I nodded. From downstairs there came the sound of a flop—the noise that a letter box makes when someone pushes letters through.

She got up. "There is the post, M'sieu." She began to move towards the door.

I said: "Don't worry about the post, Musette. I'll look after it."

She said: "I thought there might be something from Madame— some explanation."

"If there is, I'll read it."

She said: "Very well, M'sieu. I think if there is nothing else I can do I shall go back to my room. Good afternoon."

I said: "Good afternoon, Musette."

I went down the stairs after her. She went out through the side door into the passageway. She gave me a little smile as she went.

I went into the shop. I thought Musette was a first-class, goddam liar. I unlocked the front door; watched her as she walked down the street with the light, tripping step which distinguishes a Frenchwoman. I thought she was pretty good. When she got to the corner she turned left into Bond Street. Williamson pushed himself away from the lamp-post; put his folded newspaper in his



Peter Cheyney

pocket; went after her.

I collected the post. Two or three circulars, a re-ceipted bill. But no explanation from Madame Yvette Cambeau.

# VIII. — THE ZEUS BROTHERS

**GLYDER** arrived at half-past eleven; helped himself to a drink.

He said: "Everything's arranged at the Cossaque. A fellow called Gleethorpe—one of their richest members—has asked us to be invited there to-night with a view to membership. I believe it's quite a decent sort of place. They say the food's very good. A table is reserved for us at twelve o'clock."

I said: "Good." I gave myself a whisky and soda; lighted a cigarette.

Glyder asked: "How's the puzzle coming out, or isn't it?"

I shrugged my shoulders. "I'm beginning to see glimmerings of light, though not very much. But I think I've got the Riffenbach angle."

"Yes," said Glyder. "Tell me about it. Is it interesting?"

"I'm still guessing," I said, "but it looks to me like this: There is some sort of funny business going on over here and in some way or another it's connected with Rockie. The thing started when Hermione Martin asked Jane to bring Rockie's car to Paris. Someone knew about that. Someone knew who Hermione Martin was; what she was doing. It's all the tea in China to a bad egg that that person was Marcini, who seems to have been a very hard-bitten Soviet agent. Probably Marcini had had his eye on Janey for some time. Why? Because Janey used to get about with Rockie. So Marcini came down

                                   Peter Cheyney

to Paris after Janey; wished himself on to us at Charles' Bar; came to the conclusion that Janey was on my side; had me followed; had Hermione Martin killed. Then he came over here to report to the mysterious Yvette Cambeau, who I take it, is the leading agent for the gang in this country.

"The reason why Marcini spotted Sonia at the Volanski apartment is quite obvious to me. He had been put on to keep general observation on the Riffenbach apartment in St. John's Wood. Yvette Cambeau, who we shall probably discover is the Russian woman Sabina, had already begun to suspect Riffenbach, and anybody who went to that flat was also suspect. So Marcini knocked off Sonia, hoping to discover the truth from her, instead of which he put himself in a position which led to his own death."

Glyder said: "I see. Why should Sabina have suspected Riffenbach?"

"I don't know," I said, "but it's pretty obvious that Riffenbach was playing his own game. Remember he'd been in the German army. He was captured by the Soviets and probably given the choice of death or serving on their secret service. He elected to work for them. Probably he'd never had a chance of making a getaway before, first of all because there was no opportunity and, secondly, because he hadn't any money. So he picked up Olga Volanski in Paris and made love to her. He thought this would be safe enough. She isn't intelligent, anyhow, and she was just at the age when she would be inclined to sacrifice everything for a passionate interlude with her so-called Hetman of Cossacks. When

Riffenbach and Volanski arrived in London he was informed all about me by the Bruton Street headquarters. These people had discovered where I was living—they'd probably had a tail on me ever since my arrival. Then Riffenbach had a bright idea. He caused the invitation to be sent to me because he wanted to meet me to see if I was the sort of person with whom he could make a deal. If Riffenbach hadn't accidentally killed himself, it's my guess that he would have been in touch with me a few days after the party and told me straight out what was on his mind. This is supported by the remark he made to Carla on the night when he took her off to the Forest Hills house—the night of the party—when he was drunk and tried to make her.

"She told me that he informed her that if she played along with him she could make a lot of money. He was including me in his mind. Somehow Riffenbach had information or something—I can't guess what it was— that could make him a lot of money in this country. Once he had that, he thought he'd be safe from the Soviets. Riffenbach was going to try and do a deal with me."

Glyder lighted a cigarette. "It's a pity he's dead; otherwise you might have found out what the deal was."

I grinned at him. "I've got the glimmering of an idea about that deal, but I'm not talking yet. Let's go."

It was a few minutes to twelve when we arrived at the Cossaque. The Club consisted of a very long, underground dining- room with two bars, a hallway and the usual appurtenances of a night club. It was a good-class place, luxuriously appointed, and the customers seemed to be nice people. The manager met us in the hall.

He said: "Good evening, sir. I'm delighted to welcome you to the Cossaque. We hope you will like it. Mr. Gleethorpe asked me to take particularly good care of you. Will you come this way?"

He led us to a table in the corner of the restaurant. He said: "The cabaret starts in a few minutes. I hope you'll enjoy it." He went away.

We ordered some food and a bottle of champagne.

The cabaret wasn't bad. It was the usual sort of thing that one sees in night clubs. A pretty young woman who sang risqué songs, a Tzigane violinist. Then, when the Tizgane violinist had finished doing his work, the manager came into the centre of the dance floor.

He said: "Ladies and gentlemen, we are about to present to you to-night one of the most amazing turns that has ever been seen in the history of the world—the 'Brothers Zeus.'"

The curtains on the small stage at the end of the room parted. There were two men on the stage. Both wore evening dress, but one was sitting in a chair. The man standing by his side was tall, well-built. Vaguely he reminded me of somebody, but I could find no connection in my mind, and then my attention was riveted on the seated man... a most peculiar person. He was, as far as I could judge, of about middle height. His body, legs and arms were thin. His head was immense. It seemed almost too big for his shoulders. Also there was an indefinable and strange quality of brittleness about the man. You felt if someone were to push him off the chair he would break. He had a high forehead, voluminous grey hair, a small beard. He wore thick-lensed glasses, and his eyes stared straight before him as if they were unseeing. His face wore an expression of strange disinterest in everything.

The tall, standing man said in an accent which seemed more German than anything else: "Ladies and gentleman, I present to you my brother, Karl Zeus. Karl has the most amazing mind in the world. It works with the most extraordinary rapidity. We shall show you."

They showed us. Karl Zeus certainly had the most amazing mind. He added up impossible sums in a flash of a second. His feats of memory were amazing. One of the tricks they performed was to give a number of at least five or six digits to every person seated in the restaurant. The manager went round and read each one of these numbers out once. There were thirty-five numbers read out and, almost before the manager had replaced the last numbered paper, Karl had added the sum total and spoke it in a peculiarly dull voice to the audience. I came to the conclusion that Karl must have one hell of a brain.

When the turn finished the orchestra began to play. People went on the dance floor; danced. The restaurant was exquisitely lighted. The women's dresses, the atmosphere, the good band, made a pleasant background. The manager came over.

He said: "I hope you have enjoyed the show, gentlemen."

I said: "I think it was the most amazing turn, that 'Zeus Brothers.'"

He said: "It is a great pity I cannot keep them here.

They were supposed to be here until the end of next week but, apparently, they have another contract which had been overlooked. I have to let them go."

"That's a great pity," I said. "I should have liked to see them again."

He said: "I'm not certain, but I believe they're going back to Germany. Would you like me to find out?"

I said: "No thanks..."

We finished our bottle of champagne and left.

It was one o'clock when we arrived back at my apartment. Glyder opened a fresh bottle of whisky.

He said: "Well, what have you learned from the Brothers Zeus?"

"Nothing... except that I'd like to be able to add up like Karl. Don't you think he's rather a peculiar sort of person? I think he's the strangest-looking man I've ever seen in my life."

Glyder said: "Me, too. A funny-looking cove. He looked as if he was a little mad to me."

"I should think one would have to be mad to add up like that." I went on: "Glyder, you'd better go home and get some sleep. What time do you think the Old Man gets up in the morning?"

He said: "God knows. I doubt if he ever goes to bed. I was told once that his liver is so bad that he sits up all night in that chair of his. Maybe that's why he's so bad-tempered."

I said: "You get out there first thing in the morning—eight o'clock. If he's not awake you'll have to wait until he does waken. Now describe Karl Zeus to me in detail."

Glyder did this. He made a pretty good job of it.

I said: "You go out and see the Old Man to-morrow morning and give him that description. Ask him who Karl Zeus is, if he knows. I've an idea that he's going to know that odd and peculiar face."

"O.K.," said Glyder. "If it's like that I'll have to leave to-morrow morning about five. I'll go to bed now. Good night, Mike." He went out.

I threw my cigarette stub away; lighted a fresh one. I began to walk up and down my sitting-room. For some reason or other I had felt a little better about things the last day or two, not that I knew anything much, but I had a vague idea that something was coming.

At half-past one the phone rang. It was Williamson.

He said: "Good evening, Mr. Kells. I hope I haven't got you out of bed."

I said: "No."

He went on: "I tailed Musette back to the same place in Great Titchfield Street. When she arrived there I wasn't quite certain what the form was so I hung about for half an hour. She came out. She had two suitcases. She took a cab. Luckily I was able to jump another and go after her. She went to a ticket office—the all-night service at the Piccadilly Hotel. She's got a reservation from Dover on the two-thirty boat to-morrow. That's the Dover/Calais boat."

I asked: "What time will she arrive there?"

He said: "She should be in Calais in about an hour and twenty minutes."

"All right. Thank you, Williamson. You've been a great help." I hung up.

                    Peter Cheyney

I waited a few minutes. I thought: Well, here goes. I may get my head bitten off but I've got to do this. I phoned the Old Man.

I heard the bell ringing at the other end. Then Miss Fains came on the line.

I said: "Fainits, where's the Old Man?"

"In his room, Mr. Kells. And I wish you wouldn't call me Fainits."

I asked: "What can you do about it, sweetheart? I've got to talk to him on the telephone whether he likes it or not."

She said: "Very well. Hold on."

I waited five minutes for the Old Man. Then there was a grunt.

"What the hell's the matter with you, Kells. Can't you let me get any rest?"

I said: "I'm sorry, but I have to do this. A woman called Musette Lehaye—about twenty-eight years of age—five feet seven inches in height, dark brown eyes, a round face; purports to be French, looks French, speaks French, has a French passport—that might mean any-thing—is leaving England to-morrow, from Dover on the two-thirty boat. Somebody's got to pick her up at Calais. She's important."

The Old Man asked: "Is that all?"

I said: "I think it's enough to be going on with. Can you arrange that? If so, I want to know the name of the agent who'll pick her up there. Maybe I'll be going to France myself in a day or so. I might like to talk to him."

He said: "You know the man who'll be tailing her.

He's an old friend of yours. I've always considered you two the most disreputable operatives in the Service. Behave yourselves."

I asked: "Who is this paragon of virtue?"

The Old Man grunted. He said: "Mario Salvatini."

I cocked an eyebrow. "So it's like that over there, is it?"

He said: "Yes, it's like that."

I said: "Good night," and hung up.

If the Old Man was using Mario Salvatini he was expecting a lot of trouble.

**NEXT** morning I got up at eleven-thirty, drank some coffee, lighted a cigarette and walked about my sitting-room in my dressing-gown. I was feeling pretty good about things, although I suspected the Old Man of holding back quite a lot from me. The fact that Salvatini was to be put on Musette's tail told me a lot, and the fact that the Old Man had Mario waiting in Calais for somebody to land in France told me that he was either guessing very correctly or maybe he was one jump ahead of me in his reasoning.

At twelve o'clock Horace Greeley arrived. Greeley was a strange type. He'd done some very distinguished service during the war; had taken some big chances and carried his life in his hands on at least half a dozen occasions. But his adventures had never disposed of his Cockney accent. Greeley was a thin, weedy type with a heart of gold and the nerve of the devil. He had his limitations but within these he was an extremely intelligent operative.

                        Peter Cheyney

I gave him a chair and a cigarette. I said: "Well, Horace, what about it?"

He said: "It was easy, Mr. Kells. This place is one of those small dumps; you know, the sort of place where everybody talks about everybody else's business, and Valley House is the big house, so people are naturally interested in what goes on there— 'specially as Miss Rockhurst is pretty popular around the place. But that wasn't all," he continued. "I had a bit of luck. Miss Rockhurst has an account at the local bank, and when I started nosing around there I found one of the boys working at the bank was an old pal of mine."

I said: "So that made it easy?"

"Yes. Here's the story. Miss Rockhurst has been living up there for years. When her brother was in England he used to stay there. The normal servants in the house were the housekeeper, the butler, two maids and a cook and a gardener. But during the last three weeks there's been another servant there—a sort of general secretary and valet. He's supposed to be an Alsatian. I don't think he's very popular in the neighbourhood, although he seldom goes out. The funny thing is this Alsatian fellow acts as a sort of telephone attendant in the house. If you ring up there you speak to him. If anybody wants to phone to the village or anywhere else they put the call through him."

I said: "I see. A sort of telephonic watchdog."

Greeley said. "Maybe. That's a good description. There have been one or two people going to Valley House lately—more people than usually go there. Miss Rockhurst has been at home all the time. Usually, they tell me in the village, she goes off for week-ends and sometimes a week's holiday. She's fond of driving her car all over the country. But not for the last two or three weeks. Apparently she's stuck to that place like a sick kitten to a hot brick."

I asked: "What else?"

"This is the main thing," said Greeley. "Two weeks ago a credit was transferred from London to the local branch of the bank there in her name—a big one, twenty-five thousand pounds. She drew twenty thousand of this within four days of its arrival, and the funny thing was she drew it in five pound notes. It's a hell of a lot of cash to have kicking around, isn't it?"

I said: "You're telling me. What else?"

"Nothing else. I hoped it might help."

I said: "It helps a lot, Greeley. All right. Stick around..."

"Oh, there's one thing more," said Greeley. "I don't see that it particularly matters, but I might as well tell you. Miss Rockhurst intended to go away three or four days ago. Apparently she's got a villa in the Pas de Calais."

"Why didn't she go?" I asked.

"Apparently some repairs are being done to the villa," said Greeley. "Something went wrong with the drains or something and the local authorities ordered the place to be put in order to their satisfaction. So she's had to postpone her visit."

I asked: "For how long, Greeley. Do you know when she's going?"

He shook his head.

"All right," I said. "I'll let you know when I want you again."

He got up. "O.K., Mr. Kells. If there's anything exciting breaking try and cut me in on it. I'm getting stale."

I said: "Yes. You had too good a time in the war. This peace is a little dull for all of us."

He cocked an eyebrow. "Peace? If this is peace, I'd like to know what a war is. So long, Mr. Kells." He went off.

I threw my cigarette stub away, bathed and dressed. Now the jig-saw puzzle was beginning to clear up a little bit. Now I was beginning, vaguely, to see who did what and why—except for one or two things. For the life of me I couldn't get the Zeus Brothers and how they came into this. But did they? Just because I'd found a typewritten note which had been put through Yvette Cambeau's front door, I'd imagined that this was an intentional tip-off. It might have been anything. It might have been ordinary door-to-door advertising. But I didn't think it was.

The reason why Musette had returned to the shop twice after it was closed was, I thought, to collect the post. Musette was waiting for that tip-off and she hadn't got it. So, unless she'd found where the Zeus Brothers were performing and seen the show herself, I was one jump ahead of her; that is if she was what I thought she was.

At two o'clock I went round to the garage; got out the car; drove down to Balcombe. It was a pleasant day, cool but with a nice afternoon sun. I ambled quietly along, wondering but not being at all certain what I was going to say to Miss Rockhurst if and when I saw her. I shrugged my shoulders. When you're going to talk to a woman, anything might happen. If she wants to talk she tells you lies if she wants to tell lies. And if she doesn't want to talk she still tells lies. Because you can lie by not talking just as easily as you can by talking—at least you can if you're a woman. But my own guess was that Valerie Rockhurst was in a rather difficult position. At least it would be interesting to see how she was going to play it.

I arrived at the house just after three-thirty, parked the car in the gravel courtyard before the imposing portico, went up the steps and rang the bell. I waited a minute or two; then the door opened. I expected to see the butler whom I'd seen the time before, but there was a new one. This one was dressed in a short, black coat, waistcoat and striped trousers, a very correct white collar and grey tie. He had a thin face and iron-grey hair, and his eyebrows went up at the corners, giving him a peculiar and not unattractive Mephistophelian look.

I said: "Good evening. I want to see Miss Rockhurst. My name's Kells."

He said with a definite foreign accent: "Excuse me, but have you some business with Miss Rockhurst?"

I said: "Don't be such a damn fool. I wouldn't come here to talk with her unless I had, would I?"

He said: "I don't know if Miss Rockhurst is in."

"Well, I'll help you. I think she's in and if she isn't in I'm coming inside to wait until she is in. Do you understand?"

                          Peter Cheyney

He said: "I'm very sorry but you're not coming in this house until I have reported to Miss Rockhurst and know that she wishes to see you." His tone was both uncivil and definite.

I put the palm of my right hand over his nose and pushed. He went back into the hall; landed on his back. I stepped inside and shut the door behind me. I watched him as he got up.

"Now go and tell Miss Rockhurst I'm here. And I'd like to tell you something, my friend. Any obstruction from you and you're going round to the local police station quick! Understand?"

He stood looking at me. His hands were shaking but whether that was fear or rage I wouldn't know. Then he half shrugged his shoulders; went away.

He came back in two or three minutes and said politely: "Will you come this way, sir?"

He took me into the drawing-room on the right hand side of the hall. I lighted a cigarette; waited. A few minutes afterwards she came into the room. I told you the last time I saw this woman that I thought she was rather wonderful. During the period since then, I'd often thought about her; told myself that it wasn't possible for any woman to be as beautiful as she was. Now, looking at her, I knew that my first guess had been right.

She wore a very well-tailored frock of grey Oxford wool with a simple collar and cuffs of powder blue. Her wonderful hair was dressed as before—caught back with the tortoiseshell clip. But her eyes were worried. There were deep circles beneath them. I thought Valerie

Rockhurst had been having a bad time about something.

She said in a cold voice: "Good afternoon, Mr. Kells. I understand your entrance here was rather forcible. Surely it is in order for me to employ servants to find out who people are before I see them."

"It's quite in order, Miss Rockhurst, and if you employ the sort of servant who opened the door to me this afternoon you must expect some more rough entrances. Perhaps you'd like to tell me who this man is, where he comes from and why he is here?"

She shrugged her shoulders. "My housekeeper employs servants for this house, Mr. Kells."

I asked: "Did she employ this one? If so, maybe I could see the housekeeper."

She said: "Mr. Kells, I don't understand your attitude. Exactly what does all this mean?"

I took a chance. "Miss Rockhurst, my attitude towards you is the same as my attitude towards any person I suspect of treason, which I think is a beastly sort of crime, and in this case"—I smiled at her—"it's a particularly low sort of treason because it's treason against two countries, isn't it—not only this one but your own?"

She said in a low voice: "What do you mean?"

"You know damn well what I mean," I replied. "I think the time has come when you and I might have a little talk. Let's make up our minds whether we are going to be friends or enemies. If you want to be enemies you have it your way and I'll have it mine and it's not going to be very pleasant for you. You'll find it easier to be friends with me."

                                    Peter Cheyney

She sat down in a chair by the table. For a moment she looked quite helpless—rather like a child who's been caught out doing something wrong, and smacked. Then she squared her shoulders and faced up to it.

She asked: "What am I supposed to say, Mr. Kells?"

"Just what you like," I told her. "Perhaps you might like to answer a question or two."

"Such as?" she queried.

I said: "Within a few hours of seeing me last you decided to take a trip up to town and to go and see a lady called Yvette Cambeau. Don't tell me that you went to see her about a frock. First of all she doesn't know anything about making frocks and, secondly, you went there at rather a late hour for business like that. What did you see her for?"

She said: "Surely I can see my dressmaker if I want to."

I laughed at her. "Shall I answer the question?"

She said defiantly: "If you like. Can you?"

"I think so. You went to see Yvette Cambeau to tell her that I'd called on you that afternoon; to tell her that the British Secret Service was particularly interested in one or two points concerning you and her. And you didn't go to tell her that just because you wanted to talk to her either. It was necessary that you went to see her to entreat her to get a ripple on with the particular business you two have in hand, because you thought if she didn't get a move on it was going to be too late. Well, am I right or wrong?"

She shrugged her shoulders. The same helpless look came over her face. For a minute or two I was almost sorry for her. I pulled up a chair; sat down opposite her. I offered her my cigarette case. I said: "Smoke a cigarette and relax, and listen to me."

She took a cigarette and I lighted it for her.

I went on: "There's nobody who's such a complete damn fool as a woman when she is a damn fool, because she seldom knows she's being a damned fool. Men are inclined to run the more dangerous businesses in their lives with their heads." I grinned at her. "Women on the contrary are only dangerous when they're using their hearts and you couldn't be dangerous. You're not the sort of woman who should even try to be." I shot a quick question at her. "When, where and why, did you give that twenty thousand pounds in cash to Riffenbach or Alexandrov as he called himself?"

She sat bolt upright. I could see her long fingers clench. I'd hit the nail on the head. "Well," I went on, "that's another question you don't like to answer, isn't it? Listen to me, Miss Rockhurst, you're what is commonly called stupid. Did you believe Riffenbach? If you did, you're a fool. And I'm going to tell you something. Whatever Riffenbach promised to do for that twenty thousand pounds he's not going to be able to do it. He couldn't do it if he wanted to."

She asked in a hoarse voice: "What do you mean, Mr. Kells?"

I said: "Riffenbach's dead. This is how much good he is to you."

Her hands clenched again. She said: "Oh, my God...!"

I got up: I asked: "Do you know what I think you

                    Peter Cheyney

are? I think you're a stupid little fool. A beautiful one but still a fool. Why ever did you think you could stick your neck into something like this and get away with it? Was it because you had an idea that the Service to which I belong is rather an indifferent one? Or perhaps you thought it was fun? In any event you might have been decent enough to remember your brother Rockie. I hope I'm a better friend to him than you are a sister."

She got up. She said: "How dare you say that to me, Mr. Kells?"

I laughed at her. "Why not? You make a pretty picture of injured dignity, but for two pins I'd put you across my knee and smack you. At the present moment you make me sick."

She said: "Is that all you have to say to me?" I could see the tears in her eyes. She was fighting to keep them back.

I said "No." I tried another fast one. "As the proprietress of this house you're responsible for the servants in it. Have you the National Insurance card and have you seen the passport of the alien who opened the door to me?"

She said: "No..."

I asked: "Have his papers been seen by your housekeeper or your butler—the English one?"

"No... I engaged the Alsatian."

"Nuts!" I said. "He engaged himself, didn't he? Just one more question—you were leaving for your Villa in the Pas de Calais a few days ago. Why has your visit been postponed?"

She said: "There's quite an innocent reason for that.

There's been some trouble with the foundations at the Villa. The local authorities have made complaints about the drains. They are being put right. Directly they are ready I shall go out there."

I said: "You'll go out there when I want you to go out there and not before. Now let you and me understand each other, Miss Rockhurst. You're going to stay in this house, and everyone else in the house at the moment, including your Alsatian butler, is going to stay here, too. Understand that I mean business. This house is being put under police observation to-night. Any attempt on your part or anyone else here to leave this place—to go out of the precincts of the village—will result in your immediate arrest."

She made a last attempt to be dignified. She asked: "On what charge, Mr. Kells?"

I smiled at her. "I don't have to give you a charge, sweetheart. If you're arrested it will be under the Defence of the Realm Act. If your brother Rockie ever hears of that he'll be awfully pleased with you, won't he?"

She said nothing.

I concluded: "Well, now at last we understand each other. You're going to see a lot of me, Miss Rockhurst—maybe to-morrow, maybe the next day, maybe some other time—but until you do see me in person, and get your instructions from me, be careful. You understand?"

She nodded.

I said: "Good afternoon to you."

I went out of the room. As I closed the door I looked through the crack. She was sitting at the table, her head between her hands. I could see her shoulders shaking.

I thought: You poor little bitch! For the moment I was tempted to go back.

Then I changed my mind. People who start something must learn to finish it.

**I GAVE** myself a good dinner at the Berkeley Grill. Really, I suppose, it was a sort of celebration, although I wasn't quite certain that I had anything to celebrate yet. But I was definitely on the way.

I walked from Piccadilly towards my apartment, wondering just how stupid Valerie Rockhurst had been; what she had actually done. There was no doubt that she had been playing some peculiar game. There was a definite connection between Riffenbach and herself. Well, that was easy. Riffenbach wanted to break away from the Russians and he wanted money. He'd taken Volanski for a certain amount but that wasn't enough. So he'd switched over to Valerie Rockhurst and she'd paid him twenty thousand pounds in cash. For what?

Ostensibly, such a payment would be for information about Rockie, or what was more likely a definite attempt to secure his release. But how was this to be arranged. How did they expect to do it? Yet, I took it that Riffenbach must have had some sort of evidence of his ability to do something. After all, twenty thousand pounds is a lot of money.

I arrived at the flat, and was just pouring myself a whisky and soda, when the telephone bell rang. It was Miss Fains. I wondered what had happened. If it was the Old Man, it was something urgent because he hated using the telephone.

She said: "Is that you, Mr. Kells?"

I said: "Yes, Fains... what goes on?"

"He wants you. Hold on. I'll put you through."

The Old Man's voice came gruffly over the telephone. I thought he didn't sound as bored as usual. He asked: "Is that you, Kells? Glyder's been down here. He's given me a description of a friend of yours—somebody you both saw last night. I suppose you've never heard of Professor Adolfus Auerstein?"

I said: "Have I! That was the German scientist the Russians were looking for—the one they couldn't find—the one who had been spirited out of Berlin?"

He said: "Correct. They wanted Auerstein particularly, you remember. He knew more about atomic energy than any of them did. They were fearfully annoyed because they couldn't find him."

I said: "Yes. So what?"

He went on: "It may interest you to know that the mind and memory expert of the Zeus Brothers is the same man—Adolfus Auerstein."

I whistled. I got it.

He asked: "Does that help you?"

I said: "It helps me plenty. Now I know what I'm doing."

He chuckled. "I wonder..."

I said: "Look, will you be at home to-night?"

He grunted. "I suppose so, although I've told you I don't like you hanging about here."

"If you don't," I said, "you'd better come up here now. I think I can see the story. We've got to get cracking."

                                        Peter Cheyney

He said: "Yes, you'll have to do something like that, won't you? All right, come down."

I said: "Very well." I hung up.

I began to walk up and down my sitting-room. I had a peculiar feeling of excitement—a feeling that told me that we were coming near to the end of this business. So one of the Zeus Brothers was Adolfus Auerstein—the scientist that the Russians would have paid any money to get their fingers on. And here he was perambulating around London in a night club act.

Another idea came to me. The other partner in the act—the man who had announced him! This man had reminded me of someone. Now I knew who he reminded me of. He reminded me of Riffenbach. I felt that I'd lay all the tea in China that this second man was Riffenbach's brother or some near relative. I grinned to myself. Now I knew what Riffenbach had sold Valerie Rockhurst. The whole thing was plain.

I sat down and cooled off. Even if I could guess what was going to happen I didn't know when it was going to happen or where. Maybe Valerie Rockhurst could supply this information, but I doubted it.

I sat there conning over the whole of this business from the beginning, from the time I'd attended the weird cocktail party at Madame Volanski's—of Riffenbach's talk with Carla, of his taking her to the house at Forest Hills, of his death, of the letter from the mysterious Sabina that I'd found in his pocket.

I sat upright in my chair and whistled again. That letter! What a mug I'd been. If my ideas were right, Sabina was Riffenbach's boss. She was in charge of the operation over here. She'd suspected Riffenbach of disloyalty. She'd sent him the letter—the affectionate letter signed Sabina that I'd found on him—which was no doubt intended to be some sort of warning to watch his step.

But why should she do that? She could have rung him and told him that. No one could have understood what the conversation was about. Therefore, that letter had meant something else, and like a damn fool I'd put it away, thinking that I'd extracted all the information that I could from it.

I walked across to the bureau; unlocked the drawer; took out the letter. I read it carefully. Ostensibly, it was a rather affectionate but somewhat chiding letter. It took Riffenbach to task for his dilatory attitude towards her. It pointed out that it was some days since she'd seen or heard from him. She hoped he was not too busy or that his mind was not "moving in other directions." She hoped and expected, because of the great love that was between them, that she would hear from him within the next day or so.

The letter went on to say that she considered he owed her a lot and she would hate to come to the conclusion that he had deluded her in any way, but she felt certain that something had happened. She desired to see him and hear his own explanation.

I went to the telephone and rang Woldingham. I was lucky to find him in his office. When he came on the line I said: "Look, Woldingham, this is Kells. I've a letter here. It may be in code. It looks pretty innocent but one never knows. Have you somebody who can deal

                                          Peter Cheyney

with it right away?"

"Is it in English?" he asked.

"Yes," I said. "But that doesn't mean a thing. It might be coded through another language."

He said: "Could you make a guess at the other language."

"Yes... Russian..."

He said: "Well, if you let me have the letter at once I've got a man who'll work on it but, you know, this business sometimes takes a long time."

I said: "I know that, but I'll have to chance it. If you let me have a motor cycle messenger straight away I'll send the letter back to you."

"Do that," he said. "I'll put my man on to it at once."

I said: "Do your damndest. If you can, let me have it back before twelve to-night."

**THE** clock on the mantelpiece struck eleven forty-five. I wondered when I was going to hear from Woldingham. I realised immediately that it was useless being impatient. Codes are damn funny things. An expert can decode a message providing that the message is based on some alphabetical twist; otherwise it may take hours or days. There is no code that can't be traced but in some cases the code expert spends a week merely looking at the message trying to work out the key. I hoped that Sabina wasn't very good at this department of her business.

The door-bell rang. I opened the door and found myself looking at Woldingham's despatch rider. I took the envelope from him, signed his receipt, slammed the door and hurried back to my sitting-room. I tore open the envelope, read the note from Woldingham.

> Dear Kells,
> This one's easy. I hope you get what you're after.
> W.

Enclosed was the decoded letter from Sabina to Riffenbach. It read:

You are a liar, a cheat, a thief, and a traitor. However clever you may think yourself to be you will find that your end will be unhappy. As it is, at this moment you appear to be holding a winning hand. I have reported on your knavish operations and it is found necessary to agree to your demands. The package will be available on 5th August at the time—eleven o'clock to midnight—and at the place indicated."

I whistled to myself. I could have kicked myself for my stupidity over the note. To-day was the second of August and there were three days for Riffenbach's operation to be carried out.

I thought of the Old Man, sitting waiting at his house, probably wearing the check dressing-gown to which he was attached, drinking gin and cursing me in five different languages.

I shrugged my shoulders. He would have to wait.

I gulped down a whisky and soda, filled my cigarette case, seized a hat and hurried round to the garage.

 **IT** was two o'clock when I arrived at Balcombe. I



Peter Cheyney

parked the car on the grass verge at the end of the village, turned off the parking lights, locked the car and began to walk quickly up the side road towards Valley House.

It was a lovely night. There was a good moon and the lawns and parkland around the house were silvered by the moonbeams.

The entrance gates of the house were closed and locked. I walked fifty yards down the road, jumped for the top of the estate wall, managed to get a grip, and pulled myself up. I dropped over the wall and, keeping in the shadow of convenient trees, made my way towards the main entrance.

I rang the bell and waited. Nothing happened. I tried again, keeping my finger on the bell for a good minute. I could hear the bell ringing somewhere in the bowels of the house, but no one answered.

I gave it up. I went round the side of the house looking for a convenient window. I found one—a small affair that looked like a pantry window. I thought it big enough for me. I picked up a stone, smashed the glass, undid the catch and wriggled through.

I found myself in a small kitchen. I took out my electric torch and made my way upstairs to the main floor. All the rooms were silent and in darkness. I went to the first, second and third floors. There was no sign of life. The place was deserted.

I went down to the ground floor, sat on the bottom of the main staircase. I lighted a cigarette and did a little quick cursing.

You never knew with women. Even when you thought you'd got them down, and reduced to tears and helpless. Like hell!

Valerie Rockhurst had been like that—tearful and scared. But it hadn't prevented her from collecting her staff, locking the house up and clearing out.

She'd guessed that my threat of having the place put under observation was mere bluff. Anyhow she'd taken a chance and it had come off. I would have bet all the tea in China to a stale egg that she had jumped the last boat for Calais, with her favourite Alsatian under-butler with her.

I thought to hell with her. If I'd found her she might have been able to save me a certain amount of trouble but—I shrugged my shoulders—it would all amount to the same thing in the end, and if she found herself caught up in a bunch of trouble she could blame herself.

I went downstairs, wriggled through my window, walked back to the car. It was a quarter to three and if I was going to make the Old Man's place and get away before daylight I had to do some fast driving.

As I started off I remembered that it was the second or rather the third of August.

                    Peter Cheyney

# IX. — SALVATINI

**I GOT** down to the Old Man's place at a quarter past four, and nearly burned the tyres off the car doing it. I parked just inside the white gate; walked round to the side door; rang the bell.

Miss Fains, looking very attractive in a black and white check dressing-gown with the top of her frilled nightdress showing at the neck, said: "Good morning. I'm glad you got here in time for breakfast."

I said: "Don't be sarcastic, Fainits. You're talking to a tired and harassed man."

She closed the door behind me. She said: "Like hell! Any time you're harassed I'll fly a flag."

I asked: "How's the Old Man?"

She smiled beatifically. "Stamping with rage. I wouldn't like to be you."

I said in my politest tone of voice: "Nuts!" I walked down the corridor and opened the door of the Old Man's room.

He was sitting at the end of the table between two long candles, set in antique silver candlesticks. The flickering light from the candles didn't add to the joy of his expression. He was wearing a shepherd's plaid dressing-gown and there was a bottle of gin, a carafe of water and a glass in front of him. I noticed the bottle was three-quarters empty.

He said: "For God's sake... I expected you about half-past twelve or one o'clock this morning. If you knew you were going to be as late as this couldn't you have telephoned me?"

I put my hat on the table; drew up a chair; sat down opposite him. I said: "I hadn't time. I made a mistake and I had to make up for it. I had to go to Balcombe before I came here."

He grunted. "Oh, yes...! And how did you find Miss Rockhurst?"

I said: "I didn't. I got into the house through a pantry window. The place was deserted. The birds had flown, which I consider to be an impertinence. I'm annoyed with that girl. She interferes. She flies off at tangents."

He helped himself to some gin; pushed the bottle towards me. He said: "Drink some of this if you like. You'll find a glass in the sideboard. And why are you annoyed with the girl? She's doing her best."

"What the hell do you mean by that one?" I said. "She's doing her best! Like hell she's doing her best. She's making a damned nuisance of herself."

"Is she?" he asked. "Consider, my impatient friend, if it hadn't been for this girl we shouldn't even be next to this thing. I think we owe a devil of a lot to Miss Valerie Rockhurst and the late lamented—or unlamented—Riffenbach."

I found a glass; gave myself a shot. I said: "It was an impertinence because I saw Valerie Rockhurst yesterday afternoon. I told her the place was under observation and that if she or anybody else tried to leave they'd be arrested."

He grinned sarcastically. "Quite obviously she didn't believe you."

  

I nodded. "It won't make any difference," I told him. "I know where I'll find her."

"Good," he said. He sipped some gin. "Exactly what ishappening? You seem to be giving yourself an amusing time on this job, Kells."

"It hasn't been so amusing," I said. "I was rather stupid, that's all. I could have saved myself a lot of trouble."

"How stupid?" he asked.

"That note from Sabina," I went on, "the one I found on Riffenbach. It didn't occur to me until late yesterday evening that as quite obviously Sabina distrusted Riffenbach, she wouldn't write him a note like that. It also struck me that if she had been put in to keep an eye on him she wouldn't have allowed him to seduce her."

He said: "So what?"

"I came to the conclusion," I told him, "that the letter was in code. I sent it to Woldingham. It was in code, coded through the Russian language. The letter was a threatening letter. It accused Riffenbach of being a liar, a thief and a traitor—pretty strong language. Then it went on to say that in spite of his general nastiness the situation being as it was the plan he had formulated would go through. It also said that the date for delivery of the package was August 5th—that is in two days' time."

He said: "I see. You don't know where the package is to be delivered?"

"I can guess," I said. "Anyway, I'll take a chance on it."

He yawned. "Kells, you always were pretty good at taking a chance. Perhaps you'll give me the whole story."

"It's all fairly simple—now," I said. "But it's been hard putting the pieces together. You gave me the last piece when you gave me that identification of the Zeus brother with the marvellous memory."

He smiled at that one. "You might as well know that I've been able to check on the one who was with him—the other Zeus brother," he said. "Would it surprise you to know that his name is also Riffenbach?"

"No," I said. "I'd guessed that. Here's the story. Riffenbach, who was a Commandant of a Concentration Camp, was arrested by the Russians at the end of the war and taken off to Russia. I take it that the other Riffenbach who looks like his brother knew of this. He also knew that the Russians were looking for a German scientist called Auerstein. So, with the future in mind, he probably told some funny story to Auerstein about what the Russians would do to him if they got him and took him out of Germany, and he's probably been wandering round the world with him ever since doing the Zeus Brothers Act. Then, I take it, somehow he managed to get word to his brother in Russia that he had got Auerstein. He probably thought that his brother could make a deal with them, turn in Auerstein and get his own freedom.

"But our Riffenbach was too clever for that. He just sat down and waited. He'd made up his mind that when he got out of Russia he was getting out for good.

"So then they got Rockie. And Riffenbach saw his chance. He suggested to the Russians that if they wanted Auerstein they could do a deal. He suggested that they exchanged Rockie for Auerstein with himself as the

                                        Peter Cheyney

intermediary."

The Old Man nodded. "Very plausible, Kells... very plausible indeed."

"Of course," I went on, "the Russians aren't fools. They distrusted Riffenbach, so they got in touch with a woman agent—I should think she was a pretty hot one too—Sabina, with instructions to contact Riffenbach in England and see that he did the job. Incidentally, I'd take a shade of odds that it was this Sabina who killed Hermione Martin in Paris. She'd left England and gone over there to have a consultation with Marcini.

"So Riffenbach started work. He picked up an old girl called Olga Volanski. He picked her up because the Russians were temporarily keeping him short of money and she had plenty of it. They came over to England and then Riffenbach set about putting the second part of his plan into action."

The Old Man poured some gin into his glass. He asked: "What was that, Kells?" His tone was slightly less acid.

I said: "Riffenbach had not the slightest intention of handing Auerstein over to the Russians in exchange for Rockie. Remember, Auerstein is a German—a very distinguished one. What Riffenbach intended to do was this: He knew Rockie and he knew his sister, or he'd heard of her. He knew they had lots of money. So he went down to Balcombe and saw her. He told her that if she liked to pay him twenty thousand pounds he'd produce Rockie. Clever, wasn't it?"

The Old Man said: "Not bad. These Germans have a lot of brains, you know."

I went on: "He was able to convince her that what he said was the truth."

The Old Man asked: "How did he intend to carry out this deal?"

I said: "It's fairly simple. This Sabina—his Russian boss— was running a dress shop in Bruton Street called Yvette Cambeau. Riffenbach wanted to link up with the Secret Service here. Well, it was easy enough. He'd been warned about me. He knew I was sticking my nose into the Rockhurst business. So he threw a party and caused an invitation to be sent to me. The invitation ostensibly came from Madame Olga Volanski.

"I went. I took Carla with me. If Riffenbach hadn't been drunk that night he might have talked business to me then. But he was cock-eyed, so he let it go. And being cock-eyed, because he was stuck on Carla he took her out to the house at Forest Hills and tried to make her. But she wasn't playing; and anyway he was probably too drunk. But he told her he could make her a lot of money. It's fairly simple, isn't it? He intended to see me— probably the next day. He was going to tell me that an exchange— Rockie for Auerstein— had been laid on. He was going to tell me that that exchange would take place in a neutral country. That's commonsense. The Russians certainly wouldn't bring Rockie over here and Auerstein certainly wouldn't go into Russia. Besides, Valerie Rockhurst would probably have had something to say about that. She'd probably told Riffenbach that the exchange must take place in her Villa in the Pas de Calais.

"Then Sabina became a little suspicious. They'd



Peter Cheyney

probably been watching Riffenbach and wondered what the hell he was at. So she got tough with him and he stalled her by simply telling her that the deal was going through as arranged, but that he'd decided to make a little money on the side. Because he'd got Valerie's twenty thousand pounds. Sabina didn't like this, but what the devil could she do? That's what she meant by the note. It was necessary that his plan should go through."

The Old Man nodded. He said grudgingly: "Not bad, Kells. It looks like common sense to me."

I grinned at him. I finished my drink; went round the table; picked up the bottle and emptied it into my glass. I said: "You can take it from me that it's right enough. Riffenbach was going to see me and tell me the whole story. He was going to suggest that we kept this appointment for the exchange, took Rockie and refused to hand over Auerstein who should be brought back to England. In return for this Riffenbach was going to ask me for a haven—probably for the rest of his life—in England, and a guarantee that no proceedings under the War Crimes Act would be brought against him. He had quite a brain, this Riffenbach."

The Old Man grunted. "The damn fool would probably have got away with it. You'd have certainly agreed to his terms, instead of which he has to get drunk, talk a lot of nonsense to that Polish woman Carla and then shoot himself accidentally." He grinned. "There's many a slip," he said.

He looked at the empty bottle; went to the sideboard; produced a fresh one. He asked: "What are you going to do now?"

I shrugged my shoulders. "There's only one thing for me to do. That's to go on following my nose. The Zeus Brothers were performing at the Cossaque Club. They left suddenly. The Manager told me they'd forgotten a contract and had to keep it. That was baloney. Riffenbach's brother is taking old man Auerstein like a lamb to the slaughter! All I can do is to get over to France as quickly as I can." I looked at my watch. "It's twenty to five. If I can get off in a few minutes I'll get the first boat from Dover. I don't want to fly; it's too dangerous... maybe they'll have somebody at the airport in France, and one's too easily recognised on a plane. So I'll take the boat."

The Old Man said: "All right. I'll get word telephoned through to Salvatini. Where do you want to meet him?"

I said: "I'll meet Salvatini at three o'clock this afternoon, the third of August, at the Café Liègois in Boulogne. What we do then depends on what he knows. Do you think he knows much?"

The Old Man shrugged his shoulders. "I don't know what he knows. You'll have to do your best. Do you want another drink?"

I said: "No thank you, sir." I picked up my hat. "Good night... I'll be seeing you."

It was only when I got to the door that the Old Man said: "I hope so, Kells, for your sake! By the way, if things get really tough, and you have to have a showdown, Salvatini has a contact with the French Second Bureau à Commissaire Velin. You can use the French police through him if you have to. Salvatini knows where to get him. He'll have a car waiting for you at Calais. Good night."

**THE** Invicta arrived at Calais just after two. I stood in the stern gangway, watching the people on the quay—the usual horde of Customs officials, tourists and the varied assembly that one finds at Calais. Then I thought I saw somebody waving to me. Then I made certain that somebody was waving to me.

She was standing on the other side of the railway line just outside the Customs House. She was a neat, well-figured young woman of, I imagined, about twenty-five years of age, and she was wearing a very well-cut tweed coat and skirt and brown brogue shoes. She looked very attractive.

I waved back. I thought that anyway one might try anything once. Then I went off the boat; walked over the railway line. She came towards me.

She said: "Good afternoon, Mr. Kells." She spoke very good English, but I could just detect the undertone of a foreign accent.

I said: "Good afternoon. Should I know you?"

"That's for you to decide, Mr. Kells. But I was told that you might be crossing on a boat to-day, so I came here on the chance of meeting you."

I said: "This is very nice. Tell me, why did you want to meet me? It wouldn't be my manly beauty or anything, would it?"

She laughed. She shook her head. "No, Mr. Kells. Although"— she looked at me archly—"it might have been! But I have a message for you. Could we go some-where where I could give it to you?"

I said: "Of course. Would you like some lunch? We'll go into the refreshment room."

She said: "No. But I'd like to drink a cup of coffee with you."

We went into the restaurant next to the Customs shed. I ordered coffee. I wondered just exactly what the game was and how long she was going to be telling her message. I looked at my watch. It was twenty minutes past two and my appointment with Mario Salvatini was at three o'clock at the Café Liègois, Boulogne. I could do it in half an hour, so I had ten minutes to spare. The waiter brought the coffee.

When he had gone away I asked: "Well, Mademoiselle, or Miss or Senorita—or whatever it is—what about this mysterious message?"

She said: "There's nothing very mysterious about it, Mr. Kells. But I believe that you desire very much to meet a lady called Yvette Cambeau."

I looked at her. Her face was perfectly innocent. She was smiling. Only her eyes were hard.

I said: "I should very much like to meet Madame Cambeau. Did she send you to see me?"

She nodded. "Madame Cambeau desired me to tell you that she thinks that you are inclined to be making a mountain out of some mole-hills. She said I was to tell you that any little differences of opinion between you two might easily be put right. She asked if you would like to see her—in confidence, of course."

I said: "I should—very much."

                                    Peter Cheyney

"Well, that is excellent, Mr. Kells..." She went on: "About fifteen miles inland behind Boulogne there is a small village called Lozalle-le-Pont. There is only one house of any size in Lozalle. It is at the top and to the right of the main road and you can see Madame Cambeau there to-night at eleven o'clock."

I did some quick thinking. It was the third of August—two days to go before the arrangements for the delivery of the "package." Was the mysterious Yvette Cambeau being serious? Was this a ruse to gain time or make me lose a day. I shrugged my shoulders. What difference could that make.

The girl opposite me said: "Madame Cambeau desired me to tell you that you need have no fear, Mr. Kells. She suggested that if you felt that this might be some sort of plot against you, she would have no objection to your informing the Boulogne police where you were going. She suggested they might even like to call for you about midnight if you so desired." She looked at me archly. Her face broke into an attractive smile. She went on: "I assure you, Mr. Kells, there's nothing for you to be afraid of."

"Thanks a lot. I wasn't thinking particularly about my own hide. Very well. Tell Madame Cambeau that I shall be with her at eleven o'clock."

She finished her coffee; held out her hand. "She will be delighted to have your message. Good afternoon, Mr. Kells." She got up; walked out of the restaurant. She had an attractive walk and a very good figure. I wondered who the hell she was.

I went outside; went through the Customs; looked

around for the car which the Old Man had promised would be waiting for me. There it was—a nice-looking Jaguar. A man who looked like a garage mechanic was standing by it.

He said: "M'sieu Kells? I am ordered to hand this car over to you. Use it as long as you want to, and when you have finished with it, if you will return it to a garage called Germaine Frères. It is on the corner of the main cross-roads."

I said: "Thanks a lot." I got in the car and started off. I had twenty-five minutes to get to Boulogne. I did it in twenty- three and a half; parked the car on the grass verge outside the Café Liègois; went in.

Salvatini was sitting at a table at the end of the room. He was smoking a long, thin cigar—one of those things which have a straw down the middle. In front of him was a cup of coffee. There was an expression of complete tranquility on his face.

I went over to him. I said: "Hallo, Mario. It's a long time since I've seen you."

He got up; smiled. He said in his very correct, almost pedantic English: "Good afternoon, my friend Kells. I delight at seeing you again. I have ordered a steak for you. They are keeping it hot." He told the waiter to bring it.

Mario Salvatini was one of the oddest characters I have ever met. He specialised in trouble. He liked trouble. He had worked for the Old Man for the last two years of World War II and ever since. He was a clever, cool, brainy operative but inclined sometimes to be slightly impatient. Salvatini, who liked seeing a

                                    Peter Cheyney

job through to its logical conclusion, also liked doing it in the shortest possible time. He was quite reckless and preferred action to argument. To my knowledge in the second world war he'd killed at least half a dozen enemy agents with his own hands. He did not like using a pistol. He said it made too much noise. His favourite weapon was a stiletto—a ten-inch bladed affair which he carried in a leather sheath suspended from his left armpit rather like a shoulder holster. He knew just where to put that stiletto. He told me once that he had studied the human frame until he was certain of getting the knife in the right place. He said it was disconcerting to find the point of the knife obstructed by a bone.

He was tall and thin and, I believe, was slightly tubercular. His face was long and his soft brown eyes looked out at you from his aquiline features. They were strange eyes. Their expression seldom changed and I imagine if Salvatini killed you they'd look just the same, rather as if he were very sorry for what he had to do but it had to be done.

I told him about the girl who'd met me at Calais. He shrugged his shoulders. "It is interesting," he said. "What are you going to do?"

I said: "What can I do? Maybe I'm taking a chance but Cambeau may have something to say. Maybe I've seen her before." I grinned at him. "Or perhaps I'm going to meet a stranger, but it's damned funny that she should have a girl waiting to meet me like that. Perhaps she really has something to say to me."

He shrugged his shoulders again. He asked: "Do you think this Cambeau would do something desperate? Do you think she wants to get you over to this house at Lozalle and iron you out?" He smiled. "It would be a pity to have your adventurous career cut short at a little French village. It would seem to be an anti- climax, my dear Kells."

I said: "Well, you know where I'm going. Why don't you come out, too?"

He said: "I was going to suggest the same thing. But I'll come alone if you don't mind. You go and keep your appointment. I'll arrive from another direction. It'll be dark to-night with very little moon. I'll park my car somewhere and keep a fatherly eye on everything."

I said: "All right. What happened to Musette—the woman you picked up?"

"She's living here at the moment—in Boulogne. I don't know what's going on. She's staying in a small boarding-house—a place of great respectability. She goes for a walk. She comes back. I've bribed one of the servant maids in the house to listen to her telephone calls but she hasn't made any. She talks to nobody."

I said: "She's probably waiting for instructions from somewhere."

Salvatini said: "Maybe. But, you know, she looks to me like a very intelligent girl."

I said: "I'm sure she is."

He went on: "Would it interest you to know that Miss Rockhurst has arrived at her house—not very far from here—about ten miles along the road to Montreuil; then off to the left. A delightful villa. She arrived there with a maid and a butler. The housekeeper had already been sent there. I understand they were coming before but her arrival was delayed until some repairs which were being done at the house were finished. But she's there."

I asked: "What else, Salvatini?"

"Nothing else. I've an operative keeping observation on the place. If anyone else arrives I shall know. I am staying here in the town. Here is my address and telephone number." He gave me the slip of paper. "What happens now?"

I shrugged my shoulders. "I don't know. But something's going to happen pretty quickly. The fifth of this month—in two days' time—is the important date. This is the date on which some arrangement with Miss Rockhurst is being brought to a conclusion. I suggest there's nothing we can do but wait. Tell your man who is keeping an eye on the Rockhurst menage to let you know if he sees anything that he considers suspicious or important."

He asked: "Where are you going to stay? There's an excellent hotel half-way down the main street—the Hotel Jocelyn. Why don't you stay there? The patron is a very old friend of mine. He is to be trusted as to when he speaks or when he keeps his mouth shut."

I said: "Good. I'll stay there, Salvatini."

He lighted a cigarette. "Eat your lunch," he said. "You must need it."

I ate my steak. He sat quietly watching me with his benign eyes; joined me in a cup of coffee. Then I got up.

He said: "I shall stay here and drink some more coffee and think. I take it that you will be leaving your hotel to-night at about a quarter past ten. Anyone will tell you the road to Lozalle. It's a good-class road, off the main Calais/Boulogne road. The place is about twelve miles away. I shall arrange to arrive there from another direction at about a quarter to eleven."

I said: "Thanks a lot, Mario. I'll be seeing you."

**THE** village of Lozalle-le-Pont looked almost ghostly in the light of my head-lamps. It consisted of fifty or sixty cottages, with here and there a small farm building. The road had been rutted by heavy carts and I bumped along uneasily until at the outskirts of the village the road improved. The night was not as dark as Salvatini had prophesied.

Away to the right, standing within a wall, I could see the house. I turned off on to a road little more than a wide pathway; drove through the gates, along the short drive that curved round to the entrance of the house. I parked the car by the side of some bushes; stood looking at the house. It was not large, but it was old and compact, and it looked as if it might have been the manor house at some time, or the house of the local squire. There was no sign of life. The place was in pitch darkness. There was no smoke issuing from a chimney. I thought it would have made a good setting for a ghost story.

I crossed the gravelled clearing in front of the house; went up the steps; rang the bell. Its echoes jangled through the house. I didn't even like the bell, but maybe it was cracked.

I waited. Two or three minutes went by and then the large, oaken door was opened. Behind it was a hall, dimly lighted, and in the light I could see standing by the door a short, stupid- looking boy. He was wearing a very old butler's waistcoat and a green baize apron.

He asked: "Are you Mr. Kells?" His voice was guttural and he spoke slowly as if he had learned what he had to say by heart.

I said: "Yes. Is Madame Cambeau in?"

He nodded; motioned to me to follow him. He shut the door carefully behind me and preceded me across the hall, down a short passage and into a room on the right. The room was comfortable. It was panelled in oak and filled with antique furniture. It was a high-ceilinged room and at the far end, about twelve feet above the floor level, was a small musicians' gallery. On the right hand side of the door, in the centre of the room, was a gate-legged table and on it was a selection of bottles and glasses. There was a small glass pot of caviar, thin biscuits and a pot of butter.

The boy went away; closed the door behind him. I walked over to the fireplace; stood with my back to it. I lighted a cigarette. Opposite me, in the corner of the room, was another door.

The door opened. Musette came into the room. But how different she looked.

I said: "Good evening, Musette, alias Madame Yvette Cambeau, alias Sabina."

She smiled. Now she seemed quite handsome. The peculiarly stolid and slightly stupid expression which she had worn on her face when she was being Musette in the Bruton Street shop had disappeared. She was wearing a straight, black velvet skirt, a hand-embroidered

French lace blouse, a dog collar of pearls. Her hair was dressed in a fashion which suited her well.

She came across the room; stopped a few feet from me. She was smiling. She said: "Mr. Kells, they tell me that the majority of women are stupid; that when they come up against something that looks like failure they are unable to see it. I have never been like that." She shrugged her shoulders. "In other words, I know when I am beaten."

I said: "Well, that's something. And you know that you are beaten, Musette—or Yvette or Sabina—whichever you prefer to be called?"

"I would like you to call me Sabina. That is my name, Mr. Kells. Will you have a drink? You must need one after your drive."

I said: "Yes, if you'll join me."

She looked at me sideways. "Are you afraid that I am going to try to poison you?" she asked.

"I don't think so, Sabina. That would be inartistic, wouldn't it?"

"Very inartistic." She went to the table. She asked: "Will you drink whisky and soda?"

I nodded. She poured out the drink; brought it over to me. She stood in front of me; put the tumbler to her lips and drank. "You see," she said, "I am drinking your drink. Have no fear."

She gave me the glass. I tasted the drink. It was very good Scotch whisky.

She returned to the table and mixed herself one. We stood looking at each other.

I said: "Well, Sabina, what is all this in aid of? And

 Peter Cheyney

tell me, did you find the Brothers Zeus?"

"How could I?" she said. "Twice I went back to the Bruton Street shop hoping to be able to get at the post. Each time I found Mr. Kells in occupation. You got the note. I didn't. Which is unfortunate, but which perhaps makes no difference."

I asked: "Why did you want to see them, Sabina? Was it to change the date?"

She nodded. "Yes. If I had seen them somehow I would have managed to change the date. If I had managed to change the date it might be that I could have revenged myself on Alexandrov, the ex-Hetman of Cossacks."

I said: "You mean Riffenbach?"

"So you know about that?" she said. "So you know who he was?"

I said: "I know all about him. Do you want to revenge yourself on him? Don't you know that he is dead?"

She raised her eyebrows. "Riffenbach dead?"

I said: "Yes. He threw a party—he and his friend Madame Volanski. I went to it with a lady called Carla who sometimes works for me. Riffenbach was drunk. He took Carla to a house in Forest Hills. He wanted to make love to her; anyhow, that's what he said. Actually, he wanted to get in touch with me - - "

She interrupted. "The swine...! He was going to sell us out?"

I said: "I don't think so... not exactly. But, in any event, he never got the chance. One of those things happened—one of those things that can upset the best laid plans. My friend Carla suddenly recognised him in the course of the evening. She remembered him as Riffenbach—the S.S. Commandant of the Concentration camp where she had been in Poland. She must have given it away because he drew an automatic pistol, evidently intending to kill her. He tripped over an electric cord. The gun went off and he shot himself. Funny, isn't it?"

She said: "I'm very glad. Now I understand."

I asked: "Do you, Sabina? What do you understand?"

She said: "He was planning to escape. He was planning not to go back to Russia. He was planning somehow to upset the arrangement we had made."

I said: "You mean the arrangement made by the Russian Government for the exchange of Rockhurst for Professor Auerstein?"

She said: "Yes... the business we were sent to carry out."

"I don't think Riffenbach minded the exchange taking place," I said. "That will go through automatically. What he wanted to do was to get away from you, my dear. So he went to Valerie Rockhurst and she gave him twenty thousand pounds to arrange something which had already been arranged—the exchange of her brother for the professor. Whether he ever got the twenty thousand I don't know."

She shook her head. Now she was smiling. "He didn't get it. I got it."

It was my turn to look surprised. "How did that happen, Sabina?" I asked.

She said: "On the first afternoon when you went out to Valley House to see Miss Valerie Rockhurst she

                                        Peter Cheyney

was very frightened. She thought that the interference of your Secret Service people might mean that the exchange would not come off. Riffenbach, who had always talked too much, had met her before at the shop in Bruton Street. She had also met me. She believed me to be Madame Cambeau, and she believed I was working hand-in-hand with Riffenbach. So on the night of the day you saw her she came to the shop and said that the thing must be done quickly before you had any chance to interfere." She smiled. "She gave me the twenty thousand pounds. It is about that that I wished to speak to you, Mr. Kells."

I finished my whisky. She came over; took the glass from me; refilled it. When she'd given it to me, she stood looking at me— a short, compact and elegant figure—entirely poised, entirely controlled. I thought Sabina would be a hell of an operative to have working on the right side.

I said: "All right. Tell me about the twenty thousand pounds."

She said: "I'm going to tell you something. Probably you consider that Riffenbach was a fool and stupid, but yet he had something which appealed to women. He had something which certainly appealed to me. I was fond of him in a strange sort of way and I hate him only because he did not share his secret with me. He did not tell me what he was trying to do."

I said: "I know. I found on him the letter in which you said you were so angry with him for leaving you."

"You may not believe it, Mr. Kells, but I loved this man," she said softly.

I thought to myself: What a liar you are. I realised, with a certain satisfaction, that she did not guess that we had decoded her note to Riffenbach; that she still believed I was taking it at its face value. I thought: I wonder what the hell you are playing at now, my girl.

I said: "We're rather straying away from the twenty thousand pounds, Sabina, aren't we?"

"No," she said. "We've come back to it. If Riffenbach had been a little more candid with me; if he had told me what he was playing at, things might have been very different. But that fool thought he was the only person who was trying to escape from Russia. If he'd had enough sense to talk to me, I would have told him that I would give one hand to escape from Russia." She shrugged her shoulders. For a moment she looked piteous. She went on: "Mr. Kells, you can consider what my life is like in Russia. I work for the secret political police. I am given missions to perform, missions which take me out into the world where people are happy, where they work and live comfortably and have freedom. But always in the end I have to return to that place, and then one day, if I fail in a mission and I go back, what happens to me?"

I said: "It's damned funny, Sabina, you and Riffenbach having the same idea in mind. As you say, if he'd told you the truth things might have been a lot easier. As it is, things will take their proper course and the exchange will take place, as laid down, on the fifth of August—the day after to-morrow. Shall we come back to the twenty thousand pounds?"

She nodded. "Mr. Kells, I spoke from the heart. The twenty thousand pounds which Miss Rockhurst gave me is buried under the hearth in the workroom at Bruton Street. Quite obviously I couldn't bring this money with me out of England. I would like you to have that money, but in return I ask you to do something for me."

I lighted another cigarette. I looked at her through the flame of my lighter. I said: "Well, why not? What do you want me to do?"

She said: "At the moment the arrangement is for Mr. Rockhurst—Valerie Rockhurst's brother—to be exchanged at her Villa, which is not far from here, for Professor Auerstein. Professor Auerstein will be brought to the Villa by Riffenbach's brother, who has been hiding him from the Soviets for some time. Rockhurst will be brought to the Villa by one of my associates—a man who is working under my direction. They will be exchanged. Auerstein will return to the Russian Sector of Germany escorted by my assistant. Rockhurst will, I assume, go back to England. But he will not go there alive. An attempt will be made on his life whilst he is driving to Calais to catch the boat the next day."

"I see," I said. "I thought they were letting Rockhurst go a bit cheaply."

She said: "He's a very dangerous agent. The Soviets hate him. He's almost as dangerous as Mr. Kells."

She laughed, showing her white teeth. "You see, they don't like you, either. But that is the plan. They will have Auerstein, who will leave France by plane, and they will kill Rockhurst before he gets to the boat. They would have done this if I hadn't told you, Mr. Kells. They won't do it now. You will take the precautions.

Rockhurst will be saved. But you will please remember that it is I who warned you. I—Sabina—who am also being a traitress to my country."

I said: "Very nice. So Rockhurst will be saved and I get the twenty thousand pounds. And what do you get?"

She said: "I want to come back to England with you. I am taking this chance to escape. I wish to return to England. Arrange for me to live in England. I will get some work. I make dresses very well, you know." She flashed a quick smile at me. "I will keep myself somehow. My God, I will escape from this hell I've been living in for the last ten years...."

I thought for a moment. I thought: What does it matter? The easiest thing in the world is to say yes. I said: "That's a deal, Sabina. After the exchange has taken place on the fifth you can return to England with us. We might find a seat for you in the car next to Rockhurst so that if anybody tries something they might get you. And thanks for the twenty thousand. I expect Miss Rockhurst will like to have it back again. Is that all?"

She said: "Yes, that is all. Now I am in your hands."

"Don't worry," I said. I smiled at her. "I'll look after you, Sabina. You might be very useful to me."

She came close to me. She put out her hand. She said: "Good night, Mr. Kells. Remember that I trusted you."

I followed her to the front door. She opened it for me. She repeated: "Good night, my friend. God bless you." I heard the door close behind me.

                    Peter Cheyney

I walked down the steps, crossed the courtyard, which was in complete darkness: followed the winding carriage drive to where I had left my car. I was putting my hand out for the door handle when a voice said softly:

"Do not touch anything, my friend."

It was Salvatini. He came out of the bushes. He asked: "What did she want to see you about—this delightful lady?"

I said: "She wanted to make a deal with me—twenty thousand pounds in return for her safety. She wants to escape from the Russians."

He said: "Yes? You think so? Look, I have been having a very interesting time. I arrived here about the same time as you did. I left my car away out at the back of the house under some trees. I watched your arrival from this coppice. You had not been in the house three minutes before a gentleman turned up... a most peculiar gentleman. He decided to do some work on your car. He was working on it for fifteen minutes. Then I saw what he was doing, so I decided to deal with him. He is in the back of your car."

I asked: "What goes on, Mario?" I opened the back door of the car; took a pencil torch from my pocket; switched it on. A thin, short man was lying back across the seat. His coat was open. His shirt front was soaked in blood.

Salvatini said: "He died quickly. I stabbed him under the heart."

I shut the door. I asked: "What was he doing?"

Salvatini said: "Look at the front of the car. You see

what I have done? After I had killed him I went back to my car and got some string. I tied a piece of string on to the accelerator, ran it under the clutch pedal, and here is the end coming out of the window. Now give me your ignition key."

I gave him the key. He took a small piece of wire from his pocket which he inserted in the hole in the key. Then he tied another piece of string round the wire. He slipped the ignition key carefully into its place.

"Now, my friend," he said, "we will go away. I have plenty of string. On the other side of this coppice about twenty feet away I will pull the string which will pull down the ignition key and start the car. The brakes are off. Then I will pull the other string which will pull down the accelerator. The car will start off. Then you will see what will happen. He has put enough explosive under that car to blow twenty cars up. There is a fulminate of mercury detonator wired up to the accelerator. When the accelerator is pushed down the detonator explodes. That sets off the rest of the stuff. Now we will see."

He picked up the trailing strings; walked into the coppice. I went with him.

Salvatini said: "Now watch..." He pulled on the string in his left hand. I heard the engine start up. Then he pulled on the other string. The car began to move down the drive. It had gone fifteen yards when the explosion occurred. Salvatini and I went down on our faces. Then we got up.

He said: "You see, she's a nice woman. She kept you there talking while they fixed for you to exit from this life." He smiled at me in the darkness. "And they'll know they have succeeded because they will find one or two little pieces of our friend whom we left in the back. She will think that is you. Do you understand, my friend?"

I said: "Very nice work, Mario. Let's find your car, go back to Boulogne and have a drink on it."

He said: "You know, my dear Kells, I am a very intelligent man. Whilst you are with Mario Salvatini you are safe."

We began to walk through the grounds towards the back of the house. I was thinking about Sabina. I was thinking that she was some baby!

# X. — ROCKIE

**SALVATINI** came down the back steps that led out of the lounge into the little garden behind the Hotel Jocelyn. I was sitting in a deck-chair smoking. He brought a chair over; set it down opposite me; sat down, stretched. He lighted a cigarette.

He said: "Well, my friend... is it that there is nothing more that we can do but wait until to-morrow night?"

"I don't know, Mario," I said. "I have a feeling of anti- climax, if you know what I mean."

He nodded. "I know what you mean. Having regard to everything you have told me about this affair there are some questions that disturb me a little."

I said: "There are some that disturb me too, Mario. Give me some of yours."

He asked: "Why should our sweet little girl friend Sabina wish to murder you last night?"

I said: "I think that one's easy. If I attended the exchange in my capacity as a British Secret Service agent it would be the obvious thing for me to do to prevent Auerstein from being handed over. Auerstein is a very clever scientist. We could make just as good use of him as the Russians. She would think that I'd create a situation, or try to, under which we got Rockie and kept Auerstein."

Salvatini smiled faintly. He said softly: "You're not going to tell me, my friend, that that is not what you are planning to do—only you can't find the way to do it?"

I said: "I can't very well. First of all, I'm taking it, for the sake of argument, that this exchange at the moment is on the up and up. I am taking the point of view that the Russians are willing to give up Rockhurst provided they get Auerstein and, having got Auerstein, they'll proceed to take him quietly away, leaving us to go off with Rockhurst."

He said: "You don't think that there is a possibility that they will make some attempt on Rockhurst's life after the exchange has been completed?"

I shook my head. "I can't see somebody taking a pot-shot at Rockhurst before they have had time to get Auerstein back to Germany. I think that was just a little story on Sabina's part."

He said: "My friend, I have been out to Lozalle-le-Pont this morning. You must realise that the noise of that explosion must have penetrated to the village. I knew there would be questions asked."

I queried: "Well?"

Salvatini said: "A story was put about that the immense gas circulator in the basement of the house blew up last night because someone had left the pilot light on. And it did. Sabina, or the idiot house-boy, had arranged a simultaneous explosion. This seems to have kept everybody quiet." He continued: "You have not had very much chance to read the French newspapers lately. I have. There have been all sorts of explosions all over the country during the last three weeks. Sometimes one or two people have become hurt, but usually the explosions are in a lonely place. A barn has been blown up. There has been an explosion in a garage late at night when nobody was at work. There have been twenty or thirty of these things happening during the last three months and in each case they are said to be due to Communists. Does this mean nothing to you?"

I said: "Not a great deal. What does it mean to you?"

"I'll ask you another question," said Salvatini. "In order to kill you last night why was it necessary to blow up your motor car? Wouldn't it have been just as easy for someone to stick a knife into you? Remember that the attractive young lady who met you when you came off the boat yesterday told you you need have no fear of going to Lozalle to meet the supposed Yvette Cambeau; that if necessary you could even tell the police where you were going."

I said: "Yes. There's an obvious answer to that. She knew perfectly well I wouldn't tell anybody I was going to meet her."

"Exactly," said Salvatini. "And then you disappear. You are blown up in a car, and this explosion, if anybody wishes to disbelieve that it was the gas circulator in the manor house which had blown up, would have been attributed to some Communist wishing to give vent to a grievance. And this Sabina of yours goes to all the trouble of employing an expert on explosives to be in attendance at the house and to erect an infernal machine in your car whilst you are inside talking to her. Well?"

"I thought of that one, Salvatini," I told him.

He said: "You mean the repairs to the drains of the house of Miss Rockhurst?"

I said: "Exactly. This is the way out of all their difficulties. Supposing, for the sake of argument, that there

 Peter Cheyney

were no repairs to the drains; supposing, for the sake of argument, that the gentleman who fixed my car last night has also been at work at Miss Rockhurst's Villa? How simple it is. If they have an explosive charge with a time fuse attached to it, they keep their appointment to-morrow night. Sabina's boy friend arrives on time and hands over Rockhurst. He leaves with Auerstein. Well, naturally, everyone is going to stay the night— everyone who was concerned in this business, that is Miss Rockhurst, Rockhurst himself, Riffenbach's brother. They wouldn't be foolish enough to leave in the middle of the night. And the time fuse works according to the time it has been fixed for— midnight or early next morning. So they still get Rockhurst and they would also get Auerstein."

Salvatini said: "My friend, I think you are perfectly right. Something has to be done."

I said: "Precisely. But what? This business can be arranged very easily if we are prepared to ask for the co-operation of the local police; to tell them the whole story; to have Rockie and the man who is conducting him—they must be arriving shortly, if they are not already here—picked up and tailed until they keep the appointment. But if this is done the story will leak out—the very thing that nobody wants."

Salvatini shrugged his shoulders: "I agree with you, my friend." He blew a smoke ring; watched it sail across the garden.

"But for Sabina," he said, "I would have a peaceful mind. But I do not believe in fairies. This woman is a dyed-in-the-wool Soviet. She is furious with Riffenbach because he wished to play his own hand. I believe that if he were not already dead she would have killed him—after, of course, the negotiations for the exchange were successfully carried through."

I nodded. "Yes," I said, "she probably would have done that. She's like that."

Salvatini said: "I think it would be a good idea if I took a quiet look around at Miss Rockhurst's villa to-night. I might examine the work on the drains which the workmen are supposed to have done during the last few days."

He got up and stretched. "It would not surprise me in the slightest to find the drains filled with high explosive. Au revoir, my friend. I will keep in close touch with you."

He departed, humming to himself.

I lighted a cigarette and allowed my mind to run over the events of the last few days. Everything seemed quite logical to me except one thing—Sabina. This lady's attitude was inexplicable and almost amazing.

Even if she suspected that I had some idea in my head to snatch Auerstein at the last moment it would have been reasonable to wait and see what I intended to do. To blow me up in a motor car and take a chance on some passer-by seeing the incident and informing the police seemed rather a drastic measure—or did it?

An idea struck me. Was it necessary that I should be put out of the way for some other reason?

I thought about this for some time and the answer struck me like a well-aimed brick. With me out of the way there was only one other person who could identify

Rockie. That other person was his sister Valerie.

Supposing that she and I were both disposed of before the exchange took place. Supposing Sabina's representative arrived with some other man who had been coached carefully in his part, someone who looked vaguely like Rockie. Who could tell the difference. Certainly not Riffenbach and certainly not Auerstein!

If this plan were successfully carried out the Russians would get Auerstein and we should be left with some stooge that they would probably be glad to be rid of.

A waiter came out into the garden. He said: "You are wanted on the telephone, M'sieu."

I went into the hotel. It was Salvatini.

"My friend," he said, "you will be interested to hear that I have been in touch with Velin of the French Second Bureau. I asked him to keep an eye on the air-ports locally. He tells me that Auerstein and his escort arrived by plane an hour ago. They are in Calais, staying at the Hotel Grand Duc. Their movements are being watched." He laughed softly. "So it looks as if our 'D' day is arriving. Would you like to give me any instructions?"

"No, Mario," I told him. "Just stay put at your place so that I can get in touch with you when I want you."

He said: "O.K."

I went back to the garden and stretched myself out in my deck-chair. I'm pretty hard-bitten, but I began to feel a peculiar sort of excitement that I do not often experience.

Then I began to think about Valerie Rockhurst. I wondered just how much help this girl could give me—supposing she wanted to help. I shrugged my shoulders at that one. Valerie Rockhurst didn't want to help for the simple reason that she couldn't help. She'd sold out to the enemy, high, wide and handsome. She knew they held the trump card as far as she was concerned—her brother—and she was not particularly interested in anyone else.

The idea had been well and truly put into her head that if she in any way divulged anything to anyone outside the immediate circle concerned, Rockie would have short shrift. She wasn't wise enough to understand that whilst he was of bargaining use to the Russians they would keep him in cotton wool. They wanted Rockie, but they wanted Auerstein more, and whilst they wanted Auerstein and hadn't got him, Rockie was safe.

I supposed it was natural for her to take this attitude, but very annoying at the moment.

But women can be very annoying, and the trouble with Valerie was that she was controlled by her heart and not her head.

Yes, there was something about her that was definitely very attractive. I have met many women in my life, quite a lot of them beautiful, and I suppose in a quiet way I've rather got a name for myself as a woman chaser, but to me this girl with the ash-blonde hair had got something. She'd certainly got guts! I wondered what would have happened if she'd seen this thing through entirely on her own. If she'd come over to France to the Villa to make the exchange; if Auerstein had been exchanged for Rockie, what then? I suppose she thought that all would be well, and all she and Rockie would

    Peter Cheyney

have to do would be to take the first boat home. She thought the other side would be satisfied with that. I grinned. What a hope she had! Evidently she believed too much in the decency of human nature, thinking about people who hadn't any decency and weren't even human. I wondered what chance Valerie would have had against Sabina.

I thought I'd go and see her. I went into the hotel, got my hat, walked round to the garage and picked up the car Salvatini had left for me. I thought, with a grin, that in any event life wasn't boring.

**THE** Villa stood two hundred yards off a side road running off from the main Montreuil road. It was an attractive place; standing just outside a little wood, it was surrounded by gardens. It was white, with a veranda running round four sides of the house, the entrance facing away from the road.

I parked the car; climbed over a low fence; began to walk towards the house. Two gardeners were working in the gardens. The sun was shining. There was an air of peace, almost of happiness, about the place. I wondered what it would look like if Sabina and Company had had the drains filled with high explosive as Salvatini had suggested.

I walked down a path leading through the garden; came up to the entrance. I mounted the five steps that led on to the veranda; went through the open door; found myself in a small, bright hallway. Opposite, a door was open. I went in.

I said: "Good morning, Miss Rockhurst."

She was arranging flowers in a bowl on the other side of the room. Even at that distance I could see that her hands were trembling. She put the flowers down on the table; turned and faced me. Her face was drawn, her eyes exhausted, but even so she was very beautiful. She wore a blue linen frock with a lace collar and cuffs. I thought she looked good enough to eat.

She said: "Mr. Kells..."

I said: "You know, I'm rather like a bad penny. I always turn up. Do you think I might have a cup of coffee?"

"Yes, of course." She went to the fireplace, rang the bell.

In a moment a servant came. She ordered coffee.

She said: "Won't you sit down? What is it you want to tell me, Mr. Kells?"

I said: "Ever since I met you you've been a bad girl. You seem to have an idea in your head that you have more brains, more acumen, than all of us put together. You've interfered. You've behaved very badly. I suppose you haven't by any chance changed your mind since I saw you last."

She asked: "What do you mean?"

I said: "You wouldn't like me to tell the truth about everything, would you? I might be very useful."

She said: "Mr. Kells, don't you guess the truth? Can't you understand why I've done what I have done?"

"I can guess the truth all right," I told her. "The truth is that you're a damned little fool. Do you know the sort of people you're dealing with? Are you happy to accept their word for everything?"

     

She said: "They'll keep their word. They must."

The servant returned with the coffee. I lighted a cigarette. She poured a cup; brought it over to me.

When the servant had gone I said: "So they must, must they? What you mean is that you think they're bound to hand over Rockie in exchange for Auerstein. I suppose you haven't thought about Auerstein. I suppose he doesn't matter to you. Here is a man who is a distinguished German scientist, who got out of his own country at the end of the war because he knew the Russians were looking for him. He knew exactly what they would do to him. He knew they'd take him back to Russia, and when they'd finished with him; when he'd told them all he knew"—I shrugged my shoulders—"you know what would have happened to him, don't you? I suppose that wouldn't have concerned you?"

She said nothing. She stood, one hand resting on the table in the centre of the room, looking thoroughly miserable.

I went on: "Tell me something. What do you think of Sabina? You probably knew her as Madame Yvette Cambeau. What did you think of her?"

She said: "I don't know. She seemed very nice to me. She seemed in a difficult position. She's a Frenchwoman. She was asked to arrange this thing and she was doing her best for everybody."

I looked at her over the top of my coffee cup. Then I put the cup down. I said: "Do you believe that? What a stupid little idiot you are. Your charming Madame Cambeau is no Frenchwoman. She's a Russian. She's employed by the Russian political police. This charming woman had high explosive put in my car last night. She tried to blow me to little bits, so you see, I don't think quite as much of her as, apparently, you do."

Her face went ashen white. She said: "My God...!"

"If you'd had any sense," I told her, "you'd have realised what is the truth of this story. Riffenbach was the man who produced Auerstein, because Auerstein has been for years in the charge of Riffenbach's brother. Riffenbach was a German. He'd been held by the Soviets; forced to work for them. He wanted to make his escape, so he took this means of doing it and of getting enough money from you to enable him to regain his freedom."

I got up. I walked over to her. I said: "Don't you think it's very funny that you refused to trust me in this business because you thought it might interfere with your brother's release, yet Riffenbach—the man you were dealing with—intended to come and see me directly he'd got his money from you, and place the whole business in my hands in order that we could get Rockie out of this, keep Auerstein from Russian hands and generally clear this mob up. You've been a great help, haven't you?"

She said nothing. She stood, her hands still resting on the table, her head bowed.

I went on: "Do you think these people are going to surrender Rockie unless they've got to. Do you think that? You must be very trusting, Miss Rockhurst, because I don't."

She said in a low voice: "What do you want me to do, Mr. Kells?"

   Peter Cheyney

I shrugged my shoulders. "I don't know that you can do anything. I suppose the exchange of Auerstein for Rockie is to take place at this Villa to-morrow night?"

She said: "No... no, it isn't. This was the original place, but I had a telephone message this morning from Madame Cambeau, whom you call Sabina, saying that it was to take place elsewhere; that I would be telephoned to-morrow night and told where the exchange would take place."

I asked: "And you're going there?"

She looked at me in amazement. "Of course..."

"Will you tell me why that should be necessary?" I asked. "If this exchange is taking place at some place to-morrow night, wouldn't it be quite easy for Sabina to have told your brother where to go. Why should you be there?"

She said: "I don't know. I regarded that as being normal. I want to see my brother."

"I bet you do," I told her. "I'd like to see him, too. I hope we'll both be lucky, Miss Rockhurst. I hope we both shall see him. If we do, it won't be your fault."

She sat down on a chair. She put her head in her hands. Her shoulders were shaking.

I said: "It's my considered opinion that if Riffenbach hadn't shot himself accidentally: if Riffenbach weren't dead, Sabina would have got him first for trying to make a deal with us. She's not a very nice person. Killing is just nothing to her."

She was sobbing bitterly. I felt very sorry for her. I felt sorry for Rockie, too, for myself and everybody else concerned in this job. I put my hand on her shoulder.

I said: "I think you're an awful fool, my dear. Do you want to help?"

She said miserably: "If I can."

I said: "When you're informed by Sabina to-morrow night of the address where the exchange is to take place, will you telephone me immediately and tell me where it is."

She hesitated.

I asked: "Well...?"

Tears were running down her face. She said: "Mr. Kells, I can't tell you. I can't. I wish I could. She told me that if I told anybody, if anybody knew except myself where this exchange was to take place, they'd kill Rockie."

I grinned. "That's not surprising, is it? Well, that's that. So long, Miss Rockhurst. I'll be seeing you again— at least I hope so. For the moment, au revoir!"

I went out of the doorway, across the hall, out into the garden. On my way out of the room I could hear her sobbing. I thought I'd been tough, but she deserved it.

**AT** three o'clock I telephoned Salvatini to arrange a meeting with Velin of the Second Bureau. I saw Velin at half-past three, and at four we descended upon the Hotel Grand Duc in Calais.

I looked at the register. There, in a bold handwriting, was the signature "Kurt Riffenbach," and underneath that, of Auerstein. We went upstairs.

Velin knocked at the door of their apartment. Somebody said: "Come in." We went in. Riffenbach was standing in front of the fireplace smoking a cigarette. He was a big, blond man of over six foot, going a little grey at the temples. His face was thin, his eyes bright and intelligent. He seemed very composed. By the looks of him, Riffenbach had been a soldier at some time or other.

Velin said to him: "M'sieu Riffenbach, I am an officer of the Second Bureau." He produced the leather identity case from his pocket; showed it to Riffenbach. "I wish to introduce you to Mr. Kells. Mr. Kells is a member of the British Secret Service. He wishes to talk to you. My advice is that you do as he suggests. You understand that?"

Riffenbach smiled a little. "Yes, I understand that very well." He took a cigarette case from his pocket; lighted a cigarette.

Velin said: "Very well. I shall wish you good afternoon, but I think I ought to tell you, Mr. Riffenbach, that if Mr. Kells is not pleased with your behaviour it will be my very unpleasant duty to impound your passport and that of your friend Herr Auerstein."

Riffenbach smiled again. "I understand what you say."

Velin said: "Good." He went out of the room.

Riffenbach proffered his open cigarette case. He said: "I am very glad to meet you, Mr. Kells, all the more glad because I have heard about you from my brother."

I asked: "When did you last hear about me from your brother, Riffenbach?"

He said: "Some days ago—about a fortnight. He intimated to me that he was going to interview you. I hope it was a satisfactory interview."

I shook my head. "I am very sorry to tell you that your brother did not interview me. If he had, things might have been a lot easier."

He raised his eyebrows. "So...! What happened?" he asked. "And won't you sit down?"

I sat down. I said: "Just one of those little accidents, you know, which occur in the best regulated of families. I'd like to confirm a few facts with you. I take it that when the Russians took your brother out of Germany at the end of the War, he had an opportunity to speak to you before they removed him. Is that so?"

He nodded. "That is so."

"And," I continued, "you made your little plot about Auerstein?"

He nodded again. "We had an opportunity to speak before he was taken away," he said. "He knew where he was going and what would happen to him. The Russians were taking anybody who would be of use to them. What they intended to do with him I don't know, but he thought—and obviously he was right— that they would force him to work with their secret po- lice. We knew also—he and I—that they were looking for Auerstein, who was the most distinguished scientist on atomic energy. We made our plan. I was able to get away. I took Auerstein with me.

"A long time elapsed, and my brother was able to make some arrangements with the Russians. This was after they took the English Secret Service agent, Rockhurst. One of the people to apprehend Rockhurst was my brother, and some time after this was done he

                                          Peter Cheyney

suggested to them that he could possibly arrange the exchange of Rockhurst for Auerstein."

I said: "I take it that your brother was a patriotic German?"

He shrugged his shoulders. "He was patriotic," he said. "He was patriotic to the Hitler régime. I also. But a German is always a German. Now there is no Hitler, I am for Germany whatever she does, whatever she is."

I said: "That sounds very nice, but does that match up with you handing over a brother German—a distinguished brother German—to the Russians in exchange for a British Secret Service agent in whom you could have no interest whatsoever?"

There was a long silence; then he said: "Why do you ask me this question, Mr. Kells?"

I said: "I'll tell you. You are here to make an exchange to- morrow night. You are going to exchange Auerstein for Rockhurst. This exchange will take place, I believe, in the house in Lozalle-le-Pont. Isn't that right?"

He nodded. "That is perfectly right." He smiled gently. "You seem to know what you are talking about, Mr. Kells, which is strange because you tell me that you have not seen my brother."

I said: "That's correct. I haven't seen your brother, but he had an opportunity of talking to an assistant of mine. I knew that he wanted to see me and I knew what he wanted to see me about."

He drew a breath of cigarette smoke into his lungs. "Tell me, Mr. Kells, what did he wish to see you about?"

I said: "Your brother wished to escape from the Russians. He planned this exchange merely as an excuse to get out of Russia. They had to let him go because he told them that Auerstein was in your charge and that unless he handled the situation there would be no exchange. So they let him go. But what he intended to do was to see me in England; to make some arrangements with me, after which when this exchange had been effected we would look after him. He wished to stay in England and he could only stay there with our knowledge and consent."

He asked: "And what else?"

I took a chance. I said: "Your brother was a good German, as you are. I could not conceive that he would allow a distinguished German scientist to be exchanged for Rockhurst; to be taken back into Russia; to be put to work for the Russians. He wished to plan with me some method by which Auerstein could be rescued, so that we could get Rockhurst back but they would not get Auerstein, and he would be safe. Is this right?"

He said: "Yes, that is right."

I asked: "Aren't you surprised, Riffenbach, that you have heard nothing from your brother within the last few days?"

He said dubiously: "Yes, that is true. I thought I would have heard from him."

I asked: "Do you know why you haven't heard from him?"

"No..." He looked at me intently.

I said: "Your brother is dead. Surely you know the Russians well enough to realise that they weren't going to let him get away with anything. He was working in England under the supervision of a Soviet agent named

Sabina—a woman. He's dead."

He made a little hissing sound through his teeth. "So... this Sabina killed my brother?"

I shrugged my shoulders. "Who else?"

He said: "I see... What goes on?"

I said: "It is my belief that this woman Sabina, who is a very dangerous proposition, will make this exchange to-morrow night. She's already made an attempt on my life. She believes I am dead, which is perhaps fortunate. It is my belief that to-morrow night, after the exchange has taken place, some attempt will be made on the life of Rockhurst after they have Auerstein, which also means I take it, that you will be eradicated in some way, too. They have probably got the whole thing laid on."

"I see..." he repeated. He smiled a strange smile. "This isn't very good, is it, Mr. Kells?"

I said: "I don't think it's too bad. I think there is still time to pull the chestnuts out of the fire, but if we are to do this, it must be done my way. I want to know if you are prepared to carry out my instructions."

He said: "Mr. Kells, if I carry out your instructions what guarantee have I?"

I said: "You have this guarantee. If we get away with this you can leave this country and go back to Germany. You can take Auerstein with you, or if you prefer it you can return to England and take him there; whichever you please."

He smiled a little. He said: "At the moment I think it would be much better if Auerstein and I went back to your country. Will you give me a guarantee that if I do as you want we can do that?"

I said: "Yes, I give you my word."

He said: "I accept that." He shrugged his shoulders. "I mustaccept it. It seems to me that I am in a very difficult position. My brother told me that he had everything arranged satisfactorily; that not only could we arrange this business to our own way of thinking, but that there would also be a considerable sum of money in it for us."

I said: "He was right. There was a sum of money—twenty thousand pounds—but somehow, my friend, it has got into the wrong hands. Sabina has it."

His face darkened. He said: "I see. Quite a clever person this Sabina. I shall look forward to meeting her."

I asked: "When did you hear about the appointment?"

He said: "I heard about it here; immediately we arrived there was a telephone call. I was told to go to-morrow night at eleven o'clock to the manor house at Lozalle-le-Pont. Auerstein was to be with me. I was to ring the front door-bell and I should be admitted; Rockhurst and my brother would be there; the exchange would take place and we would leave within fifteen minutes. I believed it because I did not think that these Russians would try any funny business here in a neutral country."

I said: "You'd be surprised at what they'd try."

He asked: "Mr. Kells, what am I to do?"

I said: "This. You don't leave this hotel until to-morrow night. You leave here in time to be at the manor house at Lozalle at a quarter to eleven. You take Auerstein with you. Don't take any weapons because it is quite on the cards that you will be searched when you get to the house. Behave as if you think the whole thing was going on in a normal way; as if you believed in it. Don't evince any surprise that your brother is not present at the meeting. Leave the thing in my hands. Will you do that?"

He spread his hands. "Of course. What else can I do? It seems I am between the devil and the deep sea—the devil being the Russians and the deep sea being you, Mr. Kells. Of the two evils"—he laughed—"I prefer the lesser, which, I think, is Mr. Kells. Also, I do not dislike you. I have heard of you from my brother. You have worked very successfully against the Russians."

I said: "Well, that's how it goes."

We shook hands. I went back to my hotel. I went to bed and tried to sleep.

**AT** four o'clock in the afternoon I went out into the garden, smoked cigarettes and walked about. During a sleepless night I'd endeavoured to work out all the "mights"—all the things that might happen. It was a hopeless job. Hopeless because it was impossible to get inside the mind of Sabina. Supposing that she now considered that the best thing to do was to play the honest game and make the exchange as arranged. That might be the best thing for us. But I loathed the idea of parting with Auerstein—a German who could be of the greatest use to English science—and watching this poor old man being taken away to Russia and a lifetime of serfdom. I thought that maybe something could be done about that.

I sat down in a deck-chair. I came to the conclusion that there was nothing to be done. All I could do was to wait and see what happened. But I felt very depressed.

Then Salvatini came down the steps into the garden. He was smiling. He looked as if he hadn't a care in the world. He lighted a cigarette; indulged in a fit of coughing which shook him vitally.

He said: "Well, what do you think about it?"

I shrugged my shoulders. "I'm trying not to think about it. This is one of those things in which I don't even believe myself. I can't believe that Sabina is going to play straight; yet I don't see what else she can do. She's not in Russia now. She's in France. She knows if we don't want her to get out of France we can keep her here. The police will see to that. But I have a peculiar feeling that she has some scheme on."

Salvatini nodded. He sat down on the grass. He said: "I think that myself. I think also that this woman is very clever. She is clever because she does the most outrageous things as a matter of course. Only clever people do that. Also she is determined. She is cunning. I have an idea in my head—I don't know whether it will be of any use to you; it might be. I suggest that when it is dark to-night—at half-past nine or ten—I will go out to the manor house at Lozalle. I will approach it from the back way, very discreetly. I will see what I can find. Perhaps something will turn up. But it is better than sitting around and doing nothing."

I said: "All right, Mario. Do that. It will amuse you, anyway."

"And then?" he queried.

"Be back here to-night at twenty-past ten," I told him. "Not later. Then"—I grinned at him—"we'll keep

        Peter Cheyney

our appointment."

He said: "Very well, Mike. Au revoir. Good luck to you." He went off.

I went into the hotel. I went to the bar and drank brandy and soda. I was disappointed—not particularly happy. I wondered what the hell the Old Man would have to say to me if something went wrong. I thought I knew. I'd probably be relegated to helping Miss Fains with the filing system.

When I'd had enough brandy I went to my room, lay down on the bed and went to sleep.

**I WAS** waiting in the hall when Salvatini arrived. I took one look at his face and saw that he had something to tell me.

He said: "One quick drink, my friend, before we go. I have some news for you."

We went into the bar.

He said: "This Sabina is a strange woman. She is really unique. She does something and you think that because she has done it once she won't do it again. So she does it again just to delude you, see?"

"Would you mind telling me what you're talking about?" I asked. I poured out some brandy.

He said: "She believes in blowing people up, this woman. Consider... she plans to blow you up in your motor car, which is a sensible thing because after the explosion there is no evidence. And she is going to blow somebody up to-night."

I asked: "What the hell do you mean?"

He said: "I arrived there about an hour and a half ago.

I got over the wire fence at the back. I wandered about the undergrowth—you know, the tangled bushes in the coppice that surrounds the house. I stumbled across something. What do you think it was? It was a land line. I followed it, and then inside the wood I found it. Hidden in some thick bushes was a detonator set—an electric plunger set used to detonate mines. I followed it right the way to the house. It is run underneath a door at the back. You see, my friend, your idea was right..."

I said: "I see. What she intends to do is to make the exchange; then something happens which keeps Rockie and his sister in the house. Then she gets out and somebody blows the house up. Very nice."

"That is the idea," he said. "But of course it is not going to happen."

"No," I replied. "Definitely not."

He went on: "I think it might be necessary to have a little assistance. I have asked Velin to be standing by with eight or nine selected men from his Bureau at the cross-roads a half a mile from the house. I did not tell him what for. I told him just to stay there until he heard from one of us."

I said: "Good. Wait for me a moment, and then we will go."

I went quickly up to my room; put my Luger in my pocket. Then I rejoined Salvatini in the hall.

I said: "Come on, Mario. This is going to be an interesting night."

When we arrived at the road that ran past the house at Lozalle, we left the car in the shadow of a hedge; walked quietly along the road; got over the wire fence;

 

took a little pathway that skirted the wood. We walked, Salvatini leading the way, softly through the undergrowth. Suddenly he put his hand on my shoulder. He said: "Look..."

I strained my eyes through the darkness. Then I saw it. Behind a tree which concealed it from the house was the plunger set that Salvatini had told me about, and beside it was the boy who had opened the door to me at the house when I had called to see Sabina. He was sitting on the ground, still wearing his baize apron. He had something clasped in his left hand. I crept a little nearer. I saw it was a watch.

Salvatini drew alongside the boy. He nudged me. In his right hand I saw the gleam of his long stiletto. I whispered: "No. We'll do it this way." I moved quickly forward. I hit the house- boy under the jaw. He went down like a log. We trussed him up, gagged him with the end of his own baize apron.

I said: "He'll be safe this way, and he might have something to tell us afterwards."

We retraced our steps. When we got back to the wire fence Salvatini said: "I have had an amusing time here to-night. I have been in the house. There is a musicians' gallery over the back room. I have been in that. I got in through a side door. There was nobody about. I went up the stairs."

I asked: "What did you see, Mario?"

He said: "Sitting in the room by herself, with a bottle of wine and some needlework which she was doing with great concentration, was Sabina. She's quite nice-looking, you know, and she was supremely dressed. She was wearing a lovely evening frock—black velvet—and a diamond necklace." He grinned at me in the darkness. "If I were not so frightened of her I would have wanted to make love to her."

I said: "You'd be better off with a snake, Mario."

"Come with me," he said. "But for God's sake be quiet."

I looked at my watch. It was five minutes to eleven. I followed Salvatini as he made his way carefully through the coppice, keeping in the shadows as we came to the lawn at the back of the house. We reached the side door. He opened it. Inside, there was complete and utter darkness. We stood listening. We could hear nothing.

Salvatini motioned me to follow him. We went along a short passageway, turned to the left and began to climb a flight of circular stairs. At the top we walked a little way in the darkness; then inch by inch Salvatini opened a door. We could see light on the other side. Then he slipped through the door and I followed him. We stood in the musicians' gallery above the main room, with our backs pressed to the wall. We waited for a few moments; then I looked.

Below, sitting round the table in the centre of the floor, were Riffenbach, Auerstein, Rockie and his sister Valerie. Standing up, leaning against the wall opposite them, was Sabina. In her hand she held a glass of champagne.

Then she spoke. She said: "Ladies and gentlemen, to-night is an auspicious occasion which we should all celebrate. Mr. Rockhurst has joined his sister, and Mr. Kurt Riffenbach—brother of my one-time colleague—has kept his word and produced for us Professor Auerstein. Let us drink each other's health."

She drank some champagne. Then I saw that the four at the table also had glasses. Rockie took a drink—he would, anyway. The others made no move towards the glasses on the table.

Sabina went on: "This has been a very difficult and rather complicated operation, but it was made even more complicated by the interference of a gentleman named Kells. It was quite obvious to me that the late Mr. Kells did not trust me." She smiled a little grimly. "He was a most distrustful person and I suppose he had the idea in his head that it would not be consistent with my character for me to allow Mr. Rockhurst to go away in safety after Professor Auerstein was in my hands.

"And, ladies and gentlemen, I thought exactly the same about him. If Rockhurst was in his hands I did not think that Mr. Kells would be content to allow me to go quietly away with Professor Auerstein. Therefore, what could I do? My motto has always been all or nothing, and as on this occasion, I could not get all, then nobody will have anything."

Her voice changed. Her tone was grim, menacing. She went on: "I drink your health, ladies and gentlemen, because we are all about to die. I consider this the best way to carry out my assignment. This house is mined. Professor Auerstein might be of use to my country if he were alive. He will still serve a useful purpose if he is dead because if he cannot work for us he can work for nobody. Mr. Rockhurst, too, will join us, and his stupid sister; Mr. Kurt Riffenbach must also pay the price of his brother's perfidy—this German who tried to sell me out. And because it is necessary, I shall go with you. I shall join you, my friends, in this funeral pyre."

She looked at her wrist-watch. "You see I have dressed for this occasion. The time is now fourteen minutes past eleven. Within the next ten seconds this house and all of us will be blown to smithereens."

She leaned against the wall, completely relaxed. The four people sat motionless round the table.

I took the Luger out of my pocket, vaulted over the edge of the balcony; arrived in a heap on the floor.

Rockie said: "My God... Kells...!"

I got up. I showed her the gun.

I said: "Sabina, you're a little unfortunate. The gentleman who was going to detonate your mine is trussed up like a fowl. He is not going to do anything except talk when I make him talk."

She stood leaning against the wall, her eyes glittering. Then she said something to me—not very pleasant.

Salvatini arrived through the main doorway.

I said: "Mario, tie this lady up—and anybody else you find in the house. Tie her to one of those chairs. Then you'd better go out and find Velin. You can hand her over to him for to-night. And the house-boy we left in the coppice."

I went on: "Ladies and gentlemen, this little adventure is over. Rockie, take your sister. Go out the back way. You'll find a car on the road. Get in it and stay there until we join you."

He said: "O.K., Mike. I can't tell you how glad I am to see you again."

                                   Peter Cheyney

I said: "I bet. We'll talk about that later."

Salvatini moved over to Sabina. He said: "Will you come and sit down, Madame, or would you like me to stick this knife into you?" He showed her the knife.

She called him a foul name.

He said: "I've been called worse things than that in my life, but not by a lady so beautifully dressed as you." He seized her by the arm, pushed her—in spite of her struggles—into a high- backed chair. She sat there like a deflated balloon. Salvatini tied her into the chair with bell hangings and curtain cords.

I went over. I said to her: "You know, Sabina, you are without dignity. I expect you are very surprised to see me, aren't you? The bits of humanity you found outside after the car explosion were the remains of the gentleman you employed to blow me up."

She said nothing. Her face was dead white, her eyes venomous, looking straight in front of her.

Kurt Riffenbach, who had watched the scene calmly, saying nothing, got up. He said: "I congratulate you, Mr. Kells. This is a fitting denouement to this great adventure."

I said to Rockhurst: "Get out of here, and take Valerie with you. Mario will show you where the car is. Riffenbach, bring the Professor and come with me."

Salvatini, Rockie and his sister went out by the back door.

I said to Sabina: "Au revoir, Sabina, I expect we'll meet again. It is a great pleasure knowing you."

Followed by Riffenbach and Auerstein I went through the hall. There was no one in the rooms leading off it. Quite obviously, Sabina had arranged her finale carefully; had cleared the house first. We went down the steps into the night air.

I walked round the house, through the coppice. I said to Riffenbach: "What she said was true. She was prepared to sacrifice herself to make a certainty of Auerstein and Rockhurst. Look."

In front of us was the plunger set. Riffenbach looked at it. Then he took out his cigarette case and lighted a cigarette.

He said: "She was a very clever woman. She had ideals. She believed in what she was doing. She was prepared to kill herself." He shrugged his shoulders. "That pleases me very much. But she also killed my brother. Let her have her funeral pyre... !"

He jumped forward and, before I could move, pressed down the plunger of the detonator set. There was a second's pause. Then the manor house at Lozalle-le-Pont went up in the air with a reverberating crash. Riffenbach, Auerstein and I were thrown on our faces. When I sat up nothing remained of the place except one broken wall and a cloud of fine dust.

I looked at Riffenbach. He was sitting up, leaning against a tree, smiling. I shrugged my shoulders.

After all, it seemed to me the best ending.

# XI. — VALERIE

**I STOPPED** the car in Bruton Street; walked up the little lane; opened the side door and went into the shop of the late Yvette Cambeau. A thin film of dust was over everything. The place looked strange and deserted. I wondered if ghosts would walk there.

I went into the back room, pulled back the carpet from the fireplace; examined it. The tile in front of the fireplace was easy to remove. I took it out. Underneath, in a cavity actually below the grate, was an oilskin package. I opened it. Inside, was the twenty thousand pounds in fivers. I grinned to myself.

So Sabina had told me the truth. Because she thought I would never know it was the truth; that I'd be dead within a few minutes of her telling it, she hadn't bothered about lying. I replaced the tile and the carpet; picked up the oilskin package. I went out, got into my car and drove home, the way I had come.

**AT** four o'clock the telephone rang. It was Rockie.

He said: "Are you coming down here, Michael?"

I asked: "Why should I?"

He said: "My sister wants to talk to you. She thinks she owes you a lot of explanation."

"I never listen to women's explanations," I replied. "They're usually very difficult and rather untrue."

He said: "Well, you'd better speak to her."

She came on the line. She said: "I wish you'd come

down here, Mr. Kells. I want to see you... really!"

I said: "I was coming down in any event. I have found some money that belongs to you—the twenty thousand pounds you gave Sabina."

"I was very stupid, wasn't I?" she said. "I'd much better have saved my money and talked to you."

I said: "Maybe. But women are strange things, you know."

"So I've heard," she said. "I particularly want you to come down, Mr. Kells. Will you come to dinner?"

"With pleasure. But why do you want me to come, particularly?" I asked.

She said: "I'd like to show you just how strange women can be."

**THE END**

A story from

Stories reflecting today
Yabot AB
www.yabot.se

     Peter Cheyney

**Dressed to Kill** is Peter Cheyney's best selling
story of murder in London's West End
Available in print, and as e-book and audiobook
from Yabot